Lock Down Publications and Ca$h
Presents

I0664168

NO TIME FOR

ERROR

Get It How U Live

By
KEESE

First Edition 2023

Printed in the United States of America

Lock Down Publications
P.O. Box 944
Stockbridge, GA 30281
www.lockdownpublications.com

Like our page on Facebook: Lock Down Publications
www.facebook.com/lockdownpublications.ldp

Stay Connected with Us!

Text **LOCKDOWN** to 22828 to stay up-to-date with new releases, sneak peaks, contests and more…

Like our page on Facebook:
Lock Down Publications

Join Lock Down Publications/The New Era Reading Group

Visit our website:
www.lockdownpublications.com

Follow us on Instagram:
Lock Down Publications

Email Us: We want to hear from you!

Chapter 1

Snatch pulled up at the entrance gate of The Residence apartment complex and inserted a code to a keypad to gain access to the gated community. He then glanced at his wristwatch noticing the time: 9:02PM. The gate that encircled the middle-class community slowly opened as he pulled in and cruised through the parking lot, surveying his surroundings. He brought the stolen F-250 to a halt beside a tuxedo BMW M6 coupe. He then exited the Ford, along with Malik and Castro, as the engine idled quietly in park. All three masculine figures were dressed in black army fatigue pants with the word DEA stitched across the front of their black tee shirts in bold, yellow letters. Their faces were covered with black ski masks, concealing their identities as black gloves covered their hands.

As they approached their designated section of the perfectly aligned apartment, Castro removed his cell phone from his left cargo pocket, placing a call to their next victim. On the fourth ring, just as an enticing female voice answered the phone, Castro kicked in the door, busting the lock and splintering wood into the apartment.

Joel stood frozen, in shock, as she dropped the phone. "Please don't shoot," she begged as she stood paralyzed with fear, wearing only a towel wrapped around her body that she had grabbed while sprinting from the shower to answer the phone.

"Shut up, bitch!" Barked one of the masked men, smacking her violently across the face with the barrel of his gun.

4

The brutal force bruised the left side of her cheek, leaving her traumatized and confused as she wondered for a moment if the men were actually federal agents.

Snatch smacked her a second time just off G.P. with the back of his hand like Blue Face on a bad night. "Bitch, where that bag at?" He demanded.

Her consciousness was slipping until Snatch grabbed her by the hair and drew his hand to slap her once more. She mumbled a few words.

"What, bitch?" He insisted.

Before she could utter another word, Castro interrupted. "She said some'em bout a closet." He replied, glancing over to the closet, which was full of designer clothing. From the looks of it, you could tell whoever's condo this was, was getting real money.

Although Joel had a bruised cheek with blood trickling down her chin from the corner of her mouth, Snatch found himself mesmerized by her beauty.

She was pecan tan with long, curly hair cascading down her shoulders. Her petite body and firm breasts accented her nice, voluptuous ass; definitely Go Viral material.

As he became suddenly aroused, he snatched the woman's towel off as Castro was exiting the closet with two massive duffle bags filled with dirty money.

"We good. Let's move out," he said excitedly. Hype in the way only dead presidents could make you.

Snatch was overwhelmed by the woman's beauty; he almost forgot Castro was in the closet and their purposes for being there. "Bruh, I'm bout smash shorty," he said with lust in his eyes.

For a moment Castro thought Snatch was insane until he viewed the woman's body himself. He too became suddenly aroused sexually. Snatch threw the woman on the bed and forced his love muscle into her mouth without a second thought. She then rationalized and began sucking him off as though she was auditioning for Karrine "Super head" Steffans's life story.

"Bruh...I think shorty likes it," Snatch said breathlessly as Castro unzipped his jeans and pulled his erect love muscle out, grabbing her from behind to probe her insides.

"Damn, dis pussy wetter than a jacuzzi." Castro moaned. Malik was losing patience standing post in the dark living room, but he knew not to abandon it, thinking and contemplating what he was gonna do with his share of the dirty money. Moments later, Snatch and Castro came walking out, interrupting his fuel of motivation.

All three men excitedly exited the condo, walking discreetly while scanning the area. They jumped quickly into the stolen F-250 and sped off as the sound system blasted trap music to their next destination.

Joel slowly lifted herself off the bed. She was terrified as she grabbed her phone and quickly dialed a series of numbers. The call went straight to the voicemail, so she hung up. Moments later her phone rang, and she looked at the caller ID. Paranoia set in as she reflected on the last time her phone had rung and her door was being kicked in. The incident had derailed her life. She couldn't believe her attackers had violated her sexually. After a few rings, she took a deep breath and lifted the phone to her ear. "Hello!" She said in a frightened voice and still shook up from what just happened.

"Didn't I tell you that I was on the way?" A mild voice on the other end responded.

"Nigga, you need to come home, now. Shit, some niggas just ran up in our shit—" she said, shaking worse than a dope fiend who hadn't had a hit all day.

"What?" The voice thundered angrily.

"You heard me; I ain't stutter. Some niggas kicked in the door while I was in the shower and demanded money," she replied.

"You alright?" He asked, concerned.

"Hell naw, I ain't alright. I'm 'bout to get the hell out of there," she admitted.

"Hold up, don't move. I'm on the way now," he said, ending the call.

***

"Cee, you just got here. Where the fuck you going now?" Jade asked, grabbing him by the arm as he began to dress himself.

"I gotta make a run real quick. Something just came up. I'll be back," he said in a low tone as he left the bedroom.

Jade quickly jumped up and ran to the window, observing him through the curtain until he disappeared into his seashell-colored Range Rover. She then two-stepped her way back into her bedroom where a Fendi bag sat on the dresser, reached for her phone, and hit Castro on the speed dial.

"Red Rum Salute. Turn that shit down," she started as the music lowered. "Did y'all see my client?" she asked Castro, hoping the hook went accordingly as planned.

"Red Rum Salute. Facts. Ma, we extorted that bitch for all dude's treasures."

"Where y'all at now?"

"Pulling in the hotel parking lot!"

"Say no more...Angel Dust."

"Say it two times," he said, ending the call.

***

Ceelo parked his Range Rover a few buildings down from his condo then reached between the seats and pulled out a chrome four-fifth. Scanning the parking lot closely before getting out, he walked at a natural pace towards the condo.

Noticing the door off the hinges he stepped inside, mindful of the aggressiveness, and yelled for Joel as he maneuvered his way through the condo.

Joel appeared suddenly, slipping out of the bedroom and rushing into his arms.

"Baby, you alright?" he asked, stroking her hair and gazing into her eyes.

"Just a little sore, but I'm good," she responded.

"Come here. How did this happen?" He took another glance at her bruises.

"One of them dudes hit me with his gun."

"Did y'all grab the money out of the guest room?"

"No, but we grabbed everything from the closet...I told you to let me put it in the safe."

He walked into the guest room of the condo, scrutinizing the picture frame upon the wall before moving it to gain access to the hidden compartment. Once inside he began to fill the duffle bags with dirty money. He went back into the room where Joel was occupied, stuffing her luggage with clothes. "Here," he said, handing her a stack of fifties like it was nothing. "I'ma be gone for a couple of days. That should hold you 'til I get back." He lifted the two duffle bags from the carpet which contained one million plus and headed towards the door, struggling with the heavy load.

"Be careful, Cee, and call me. I'll be at Destiny's place."

"Alight," he said as he turned to leave.

8

Chapter 2

"That's seventy-five thousand a piece," Snatch said.

"Yo, son, we're really good now. Ain't no turning back for me!" Castro shouted excitedly to his comrades.

"Yo, I say we celebrate. Word up. Call up the maitre'd and tell'em to bring up four bottles of Ace of Spades, on me!" Malik shouted, staring at his share of the money.

"So, everything went according to script?" Jade asked, folding her arms across her chest.

"Facts...We even ran a train on the slut bucket," Snatch said.

"Bruh, watch your fucking mouth!" Castro screamed loudly.

"Oh. You catching feelings for strangers now?" Snatch snapped. "The bitch got what she deserved."

Jade couldn't believe what she was hearing. Her circle of friends was running up in spots taking pussy. "Hold the fuck up." She interrupted. "This can't be all of it... What happened to the mil? Let me find out y'all niggas holding back on me," she said angrily.

"Nah, Sis, you know we don't rock like that. Everything is all here," Castro said walking over to the table and took a seat.

She looked at the table covered with stacks of money, pondering her next move as though she were playing a game of chess.

Even though they hadn't gotten the million plus she'd informed them about, they felt elated and began popping bottles like it was a party at All-Star Weekend. However, Jade wasn't in the mood for celebrating with her comrades as though they had just come off with some money. To her, three hundred thousand was chump change when she had to divide the profit four ways. She couldn't believe they had failed for the bait without scanning the entire condo, but *It is what it is*, she thought.

Like most diversified divas, Jade was an extremely treacherous diva at heart. Her soul was possessed by devils in the form of dead presidents. Physically, she was naturally beautiful— slim but curvy, innocent but sexy, approachable, but not easily obtainable. She was definitely a diamond. Every dope boy's fantasy.

"What's on your mind, Jade?" Malik asked, puzzled by her silence.

"Getting some real money," she said with determination in her voice. "Dis here ain't nothing but shopping money." She motioned with her hand.

"Facts...but don't worry, millions are on the way." Malik promised.

"I received that. I just hate the fact they got away with that bag."

"Jade, there wasn't no mill. We flip flopped that condo naked. Do you honestly think I'd let that bitch get away with all that money you claim was there? I'm just as hungry as you are," Malik said, looking all serious like.

After studying his face for a moment or two, she couldn't help but notice how the texture of his thick, black curly hair enhanced his mature handsome look. His skin tone was reminiscent of an eruption with a strong African effect. She could see his beautiful natural roots in him. The soft pillow pink of his lips combined with a muscular physique and Bull City swagger earned him many admirable compliments from the female population including women many years older. "Alright, I'ma take your word for it, but did you see 'em check the guest room?" she asked.

"Stop tripping, Jay!" Castro shouted." You hate to be wrong. I told you we tossed that condo upside down. The niggas was just a few steps ahead of us."

"Faaccctttts," Snatch agreed.

"That's possible, but I still think dude will help. That million y'all stayed up half the night counting, left when he left that night," Malik continued as they all intensely listened.

"Facts. Niggas don't keep millions just laying around, especially where they rest their head at. I know you wouldn't."

Jade sat silently thinking. One thing she admired about Malik was the fact that he was young, but always thought wisely beyond his years and would one day transcend beyond the limits of greatness, because he was a quick learner, loyal, low key, confident, and a gangster and a gentleman all in one. That's why she had drafted him. "That makes a lot of sense, but at the same time I know what I'm talking about. That money was in a safe in the guest room."

"Now that this has happened, do you think we can infiltrate his circle with our intentions being exposed?" Malik asked, elevating his level of vision.

"Not even with the U.S. Army," Jade answered in hopes to motivate her team.

"I hear ya, but I feel like if everybody plays their position we can get to the president," Snatch said with his shoulder-length dreads, hazel brown eyes and pecan brown complexion of eighteen years.

"Facts. In due time he gon' slip," Castro, the medium-size, muscular brown skinned felon with short curly hair said while walking across the room with the illest murder one bowlegged strut. "Shit, we done hit for a mil before."

"Facts, nigga, and gon' get it again," Snatch said, taking a sip from his bottle.

"Facts. And gon' touch that and more real soon." Malik boasted.

"Double facts. But wait 'til I grip my first mil. I'ma really show niggas how to come up mathematically. Just give me one year and me and my confidants gon' shine," Malik said, staring into Snatch's eyes.

"Malik, let us run these streets. You stay focused on your hoop dreams. I only brought you in because we needed another body to hold down the door, but I regret that shit now 'cause anything could have gone wrong. Plus, the hood is depending on you to go pro," Jade said, trying to encourage him to stay focused.

"More less, but my chances of going to the N.B.A. are slim to none. Most teams only draft like three players a year, which lessens my chances with the other players coming out of high school and college. Everybody can't make it. I can't only look at the positive, I must acknowledge the negative as well." He took a sip from his gold bottle and continued speaking from the bottom of his heart. "Life is about choices. This may or may not be the best move for me but I feel like it's my time. I gotta get it how I live today, 'cause tomorrow I may suffer the consequences. But at the same time, if it's meant for me to go pro, shit'll happen. But if not, at least I got something to fall back on. Let's be honest. In order for you to have drafted me, you had to see potential. I can carry the team to the playoffs, Jade, and in two years win a championship. Bentleys on me, baby." Malik started prophesying about the future.

Jade willed herself not to get emotionally moved by his ambitions, being that Malik was the only one, other than herself, out of the clique with visions of multi-millions, but now watching the love of money molding him frightened her because she didn't know if the change would be for better or for worse. People tend to make choices based on circumstances, pressure and their mood at the moment, not realizing with the choices they make, whether good or bad, karma is sure to follow.

Malik was Hillside High School's greatest player to ever grace the Hornets' court. Everyone admired his skills. He had won damn near every award possible in the game and held all the school's records to date. His athletic abilities were a motivation for any kid in the hood with hoop dreams. For a young man of his stature, standing only six feet tall, anyone who faced-off with him quickly learned to respect and analyze his game. Being gracefully skilled at any position earned him many awards, endorsements and championships. Named player of the year by team Sports Illustrated Magazine, Mr. Basketball of the year back-to-back, not to mention being propositioned by Reebok advertising Shawn 'S-Dot' Carter's new footwear. Averaging 32.4 points per game with 5.2 rebounds and about 3.1 blocks made him extraordinary and virtually unstoppable on the court, dribbling through and past his opponents like a maze, he received many standing ovations.

"Step aside, Jade. Let the man do him. After all, you did draft him," Snatch said, pulling Jade from her thoughts of Malik.

"Shut up," Jade said, slinging her pillow in Snatch's direction.

"What the fuck, yo," Snatch barked, looking down at his spilled drink.

"Boy, bye," she responded.

"What's good for tonight?" Castro said, trying to change the subject. "Shit, I got a pocket full of dead white guys. I'm 'bout to fly out to the A and contribute to Future's birthday bash."

"Shit, ain't shit better to do. We might as well go and splurge on dem bitches." Snatch started getting hyped. "Throw a couple stacks like it's nutting."

"Do what it do. I'm 'bout to cop a bird or two." Malik started placing his share of the money into his Louis Vuitton backpack. "What you 'bout to get into, Jade?"

"Shit, probably just lay back and see what I can find on Netflix. Why? You trying to pillow talk?" She asked while lying across the bed on her stomach.

He stared at her a moment, adoring the honey skin woman with long black hair before speaking. "You got me," he said, gazing into her eyes. "But the moment you start talking in your sleep, I'm out," he joked, laughing softly.

"Jay, you do be having some crazy ass nightmares in your sleep," Castro stated as a burst of laughter filled the room as Snatch and Castro prepared to leave.

"Bruh, hit me up Sunday. Maybe I'll be back in time to shoot your eyes," Castro said as he opened the hotel room door to leave.

"Whatcha saying? You trying to see me?" Malik said.

"Just because you nice under the whistle doesn't mean shit. I got black top on smash," Snatch said.

"The table will hold it. Make it light on yourself," Malik said.

"Five bands a game, nigga," Snatch said, digging into his pocket, pulling out a wad of cash, slamming it on the table.

"Say no more," Malik said, slamming a stack of fifties on the table.

"Yall ain't got nothing better to do with y'all money? Do you know how many bitches in the A are trying to be Superhead?" Castro said, exposing his true feelings about Karrine Steffans.

"That's all you ever talk about...getting your lil dick sucked," Jade said laughing.

"You tryna make a grand or two? You definitely can get it."

"Nigga, please. Yo money like your dick. Ain't long enough to slide through these juicy ass lips," she responded.

"Oh shit. Bruh, she tryna play you. Facts," Malik said, trying to boost Castro up.

"Oh really? I ain't gon' feed into that. She knows my number. All she gotta do is hit me on speed dial. Yo Snatch,

I'm out. You coming or what?" Castro advised, closing the door behind him.

Snatch followed suit.

Jade stood and walked towards the door to lock it after Snatch left before climbing back onto the bed. "I can't believe you staying with me tonight. Asia gonna kick your ass if she ever find out. She already think we fucking," Jade said with her thick Philly accent mixed with that Bull City talk game.

"She knows I won't do nothing she won't do."

"Boy, bye. You hungry? If so, we can go out and grab something to eat."

"Nah, I'm good, Jade."

"Damn, I love the way you say my name. That shit gets my pussy wet," she teased pushing up on him.

"Oh really?"

"Mmm-hum."

"So, what's next?"

"Whatcha mean?"

"You know I'm try'na get this money. Real money. What's good with that nigga Ceelo or whoever? I'm just try'na come up. Fuck all that other shit."

She stared at him in silence, wondering where this conversation was actually going. Even though she was on a paper trail for extreme clientele, she didn't want Malik too involved with her devilish movement because he had dreams of his own ever since he was a kid; dreaming of becoming an N.B.A. player, and playing on the Dream Team for this country. And that was a sure bank she could count on if everything else flopped. However, it seemed as though he was beginning to lose sight of his hoop dreams to follow hers.

"You say he's worth a mill, plus...we need that, so make it happen."

"Quiet as kept, it's already in motion. He gon' slip again, trust me. And when he does, we gon' get 'em for all his shit.

Come here. Let's pillow talk," Jade said, patting her hand on the bed for him to come sit beside her.

"About?" Malik asked, walking across the room.

"Bitches in general..." she said as he took a seat beside her. "But first, let me ask you something. Did you rape Joel?"

"What?"

"You heard me."

"How you gonna fix your mouth to say some dumb shit like that? That's them niggas M.O. I ain't into taking pussy, but I will extort you for that bag."

"Facts! But calm down. I was just asking you a question. Bitches ain't shit, bruh. We will do anything to sidetrack a nigga from the bag. That bitch knew exactly what she was doing, and them weak ass niggas chose pussy over a million dollars."

"Facts! That was some weak shit, but there was no fucking mil in that condo."

"How the fuck you know? Your job was to hold the door down...remember?"

"Facts! But—"

"But my ass, niggas. Just let they list take over. I betcha that shit won't happen again. Next time, I'ma suit up and torture that bitch myself, if I have to."

"You shoulda made me the lead man. You know dem niggas don't move like us."

"Facts..." She responded by soaking up his advice. "So, are we still in for pillow talk or what?" Jade said suddenly.

"It's whatever."

"That's not what I asked you." She snapped. "And stop watching my ass!" She screamed.

"How can I not when it's screaming for attention?" Malik said, sounding all fresh. "I love a woman who wears designer labels. That shit turns me on."

"Well, too bad, 'cause I'm 'bout to come out of these labels and get into the shower. Do me a favor and go look in the glove compartment and grab those blunts."

Moments later, returning to the room, Malik discovered Jade standing before the mirror in nothing but a Balmain thong and bra. "That's new," he said through clenched teeth. "Balmain, huh? I need some of that in my life."

"Be careful whatcha ask for."

"What that supposed to mean?" he asked, wanting to know more.

"Bitches are deceiving creatures. You never know who's with you for you or just because you gripped that bag and you got major swagger. The reason being is because niggas are always in the streets, and when you're in the streets you become a target. Every bitch with designer dreams coming for you. And if they sense that you're in their city and you're weak, her wolves are coming to getcha," she said as she slowly began removing the remaining of her Balmain labels. However, sex was not part of the equation. It will take more than a Bentley to date her.

Chapter 3

A month later Castro's bag had increased exponentially from all-night trapping in the trap house. He now floated through the hood in a 911 Porsche and the streets began to speculate.

"Bruh, let's get this bag. Fuck what the streets is watching. It's our time, so get in position so we can bless the streets," he would always say to his confidant Snatch. Jealousy and envy he refused to promote or entertain as he kept his path in sight, full speed ahead.

"Kaynee, take this money and get the fuck out my face," he said to one of his flowers who attended school at Central University. "Now is not the time...shit hot right now and the Feds are riding. So, go...now. I'll call you," he said, cautiously observing his surroundings for any unmarked vehicles.

Moments later a black Honda pulled aside and double parked.

Castro swung around to face the hood figure climbing out.

"Salute, gangster. You moving wet?" he spit a line he had just practiced moments ago.

"You can't be serious right now," Castro said laughing.

The hood figure opened the duffle bag he had in hand. Hundreds filled the Gucci bag. "I got a hunnit bands right now. What you got for me?"

Snatch kept his distance while trying to understand the situation. Although he was cashed out from spending outrageously in Atlanta, buying designer labels, rentals, and splurging on hood bitches, he continuously hustled. "Bruh, you good?" Snatch said finally walking up.

"Switch ya style up." Castro started speaking in code. "Duffle bag boy on sight."

"Can I live?" Snatch said, ready to rob the man for the bag and kill him on sight.

"Stand down. Bruh, ain't shit happening. Get ghost."

"I don't want no beef, homie. I just came home from doing a bid. I'm just out here to see Bunn," the hood figure said, walking back towards the car.

"Don't be coming out here throwing names like niggas gon' go for the bait. Kick rocks, nigga," Snatch said, looking into the agent's eyes as he climbed back into the unmarked car and pulled away.

Snatch and Castro were from different hoods in the City of Durham. At one point they were archrivals and notorious hitmen. Snatch was originally from the South Side and Castro was from the West End. The two linked up at Rogers Herr Middle School and quickly acknowledged they both held common interests in life: Chasing that bag and representing one another with die-hard love and loyalty.

"Bruh, I wanted to kill that nigga when he mentioned bruh name. Facts," Snatch stated, reminding his confidant that he'd kill for any nigga that represented South and Enterprise Street.

"Real facts...but you a loose cannon, bruh. You need to breathe easy fo' you catch a serious case over some bullshit. We get money in the hood. Niggas already got the hood hot killer for nutting. We got measurable goals we trying to reach. You heard what bruh said—"

"What part? He actually said a lot," Snatch questioned.

"Basically, the team will be rich by summer seventeen."

"Big facts. Y'all got that part. I'm just muscle... But, yo, did you bark at bruh 'bout that thang-thang we talked about?"

"Nah, I kept getting sent to voicemail, but Jade is with him now and she wants us to meet them after Malik's game."

"I think it's time we leave," Snatch said as another unmarked car came through for the second time.

"Yo, Snatch!" Someone yelled from the porch. "You still sitting on dem thousand bundles?"

"Yeah, why?"

"Leave dem shits. I'll be here."

"Alright, I'm on my way in," Snatch said as a fiend approached him.

"Snatch, you straight?" The fiend asked, fishing through his pockets for money.

Snatch served the fiend a gram of dope in exchange for $100, but quickly noticed the bill to be fake money. "That's how he wants to play," Snatch mumbled to himself.

Grimy was halfway down the block, running full speed as if he knew if Snatch ever caught up with him he may die where he stood.

Snatch took off, giving chase in the same direction, noticing a mid-level hustler by the name of Hysheem as he pulled out his gun while running past him.

"Bruh, you good?" Hysheem asked.

Snatch continued giving chase without responding with one thing in mind. Just as Grimy spun to face him, he caught a bullet from Snatch's Ruger, hitting him just below his heart. The sight of blood made him more violent and he furiously stomped Grimy's face into the pavement with so much force he twisted his left ankle in the now blood-stained Gucci sneakers he wore.

"Look atcha! Don't you ever come to my hood and try to disrespect me in front of my people. I should push your shit back!" he yelled while Grimy laid there leaking.

"Bruh, you know dem people riding hard," Hysheem said, jogging up warning him.

"I already know. But yo, my ankle fucked up. Take dis strap!" Snatch yelled as he passed Hysheem the ratchet and a bag of grams.

Within minutes the unmarked cars had pulled up, weapons drawn. Hysheem, however, had disappeared into the darkness.

"Put your hands where I can see them...now!" The officer yelled.

If Snatch made one false move, he would have made the officer's day. To him it would've been just another black man dead. *Fuck'em.* "I can't...my ankle fucked up," Snatch said, grabbing his ankle.

"Put your hands where I can see them...now," the officers ordered.

Castro walked over to Snatch and spoke in code, being sure to keep his distance, as the onlookers began crowding around. The undercover apprehended Snatch and yanked him up by the cuffs.

"My ankle, dawg."

"I ain't your dawg...and to hell with your ankle, boy. Now, get your ass up," the undercover said angrily, spitting tobacco inches from Snatch's foot. Once Snatch was secured in the cruiser, the undercover checked on Grimy who was now covered in blood. He then radioed for EMS as other officers in unmarked cars arrived on the scene.

As Snatch was driven to the nearest Headquarters, he noticed Castro on his cell phone. It was probably Jade he was conversing with, he thought. All the way downtown Snatch complained about his ankle, however, the officer ignored him.

***

"Who the fuck is this?" Castro answered as he accepted the call.

"Bruh, these muthafuckas didn't give me a bond," Snatch said annoyed.

"What? That's some bullshit."

"They 'bout to dress me out now."

"Word. Well, don't worry about nutting. As soon as they give you a bond, we coming to getcha."

"I already know."

"You good?"

"I ain't got no choice...you smell me?"

"I'm 'bout to pull up and put some money in your account now."

Moments later their call ended, and Snatch called his baby momma and had her call Jade on three-way.

"Hello?" Her soft voice answered.

"Red Rum Salute."

"Damn, Snatch, I heard what happened. You alright?" She asked sadly.

"Hell nah, I ain't alright. I'm boxed in."

"I can't imagine how you feel right now, but don't worry, we gotcha. I'll call Bill Thomas in the morning."

"Yeah, he may get this shit dropped."

"We gon' go holla at ol' buddy, too," she said, hinting towards Grimy. "If they don't give you a bond, I'll come through and visit, and I'ma holla at my people at the jail so you can have something to smoke on."

"I definitely need that," Snatch said, smiling as though she could see him.

"I gotcha," she continued.

"Where Malik at?"

"Right here, counting money. Hold on." She handed Malik the phone.

"What's good, homie? Red Rum Salute," Malik said, happy to hear his man's voice.

"Red Rum Salute. Not shit. Just contemplating my next move. You heard 'bout the fuck move that nigga Grimy tried to pull, right?"

"Yeah, Jade filled me in. Don't worry, we gon' handle it. Just chill."

"I can't believe that nigga tried me like that. Much shit I do for him?"

"Don't even worry 'bout nothing. We gon' handle whatever needs to be done. Use this time to work on self. He who knows himself knows how to strengthen his weakness."

"Facts... I needed to hear that, homie."

"We gon' build. Get some rest. Angel Dust."

"Say it two times...Tonya, I'll hit you back when I get upstairs."

"You better call me, too," Tonya Boo said, ending the call.

Chapter 4

Early Monday morning Malik walked over to the corner of Halley and Kent Street. He was shooting dice with some of his colleagues while waiting on the school bus, when suddenly an Oxford green Lexus SUV with tinted windows stopped at the intersection.

"You know the business...run dem pockets," the masked man stated as he jumped out of the SUV.

Everyone else stood in shock, however, Malik had already hammered his 44 magnums when he noticed the unfamiliar SUV coming up Kent Street in a distance.

Seeing the seriousness in Malik's eyes, the mask man lifted his mask from his face and revealed his identity. "It's me, bruh...I had you shook," Castro stated, tucking his twin nines away.

Laughter blared from the SUV. "Bruh, what good my nigga?" Snatch yelled as he exited the vehicle, approaching Malik and Castro.

"New day...new opportunity... What's good, though? You alright?" The young general reached into his designer jeans, pulling out a wad of cash and handed it to Snatch. "Welcome home, my nigga."

"Good looking, homie," Snatch said looking at the dead white guys.

"That should hold ya' 'til you heal up. You all out here on the battlefield witcha ankle all fucked up. Fall back and stop being so anxious for noting. Your time is soon to come."

Snatch looked down at his ankle wrapped in an Ace bandage protected by a hospital blue sock and immediately felt bad about himself. "I'm good, bruh. Bruh gon' hold me down."

"I don't doubt that, but if you can't give a hundred percent, why risk it?"

Snatch pulled with ease on his blunt as he thought about what the young homie said. "Facts! But I'm good. No witness, no case."

"Yeah, I heard they found his body in the trunk of his girl's car."

"So, what's next?"

"Cutting out what's wrong and build on what's right," Malik said.

The guys laughed.

"What's so funny? Did I miss something?" Jade asked, stepping out of the SUV, walking towards Malik.

Malik examined her from her hair down to the sandals she wore, never amazed by her dress code, as she was dressed in a baby soft pink two-piece with the matching sandals and frames that fit her face as though they were custom made, all by Dolce & Gabbana. "Damn, baby girl. You are a walking portrait of the most high-class dimensions," Malik said smiling, moved by how lovely she appeared in his presence while in the hood.

She was the center of attention and the topic of discussion as all Malik's colleagues stood mesmerized by her exotic beauty. They all wondered if she was his girl but could never tell with Malik.

"What's on the agenda for today?"

"Whatever... What did you have in mind?" Jade said, blushing from all the attention.

"Holding you in my arms, experiencing your many charms," Malik said, pulling her into his arms by her waist. "I am a prisoner of your beauty."

"Time will tell, but it's gon' take more than a Bentley to taste me." Jade could tell that Malik was infatuated with her beauty, and admired the fact she felt safe whenever around him and special when they were alone. She lifted her face from his shoulder to face him. Looking into his eyes, she suddenly had a flashback of her first love Keese. *Why?* she asked herself, trying desperately to come up with an answer to explain what had triggered such a memory. She quickly broke eye contact.

"What was all that about?" he asked, concerned.

"Nothing...Why?" she asked, lifting her chin.

"Because I'm concerned about your wellbeing."

"How so?"

"I just wish the best for you on all levels. And besides, I am hopelessly in love with you."

"Boy, bye...You're too young to even know what love is."

"You know, it's wrong to think that love comes from a long companionship or from preserving a courtship." He looked deep into her eyes. "True love is the offspring of a spiritual affinity, and unless this affinity happens within moments after two people meet, then it's highly unlikely that it will ever happen...in months, in years, or even generations to come."

"Can we please change the subject?"

"Sure. But facts are facts. I can't help I feel the way I feel. You will forever be my Valentine."

"Ahh...you so sweet Malik," she said, impressed by his compliment.

"We need to go to Holland. Can you pick me up after practice?" he asked, hoping she would say yes.

"You think it's all about you, don't you?" she asked, smiling.

"Sometimes."

"You know I will."

"See you soon, baby girl," he added, happy go lucky.

She then henpecked him on the lips, sensing everyone was watching as Castro and Snatch walked over with stacks of money they had won from the dice game. They all saluted Malik before jumping back into the SUV to leave.

"Take us to my car. We 'bout to slide down to Henderson. You wanna roll out with us?"

"Nah, I'm on my way to U-Neak Boutique. She just got an exclusive shipment in today."

**

Castro pushed his Porsche full speed en route to Hillsborough, listening to Rick Ross's album as they arrived in Timbers, a trailer park mostly housed by whites. He noticed J.T., the son of a sheriff, standing in his driveway having a verbal dispute over money with some dope boy he apparently owed money to.

"I gotcha...give me like an hour or two," J.T. said, trying to sound black. "As a matter of fact, come back in like fifteen minutes. I should have something for you."

Castro and Snatch eyed the wannabe thug as he got back into his car to leave.

"You better have my shit," dude said, climbing into his Charger, "by the time I come back through."

J.T. lead Snatch and Castro into the trailer. Once inside, he left them alone in the kitchen, went towards the back, then returned with four bulletproof vests; throwing one quickly to Castro. Castro carefully examined the vest as Snatch unexpectedly pulled out a chrome .357 Python from his waist, placing it close to J.T.'s temple, thumbing the hammer back and cocking the handheld cannon.

"Come off the rest of dem shits," he said greedily, "fo' I murder you, white boy."

J.T. twisted with a sob look as he stared down the barrel of Snatch's cannon. He stood motionless wondering if Snatch was serious or not.

"Bruh, you tripping," Castro said, reaching into his pockets, pulling out a wad of cash. "I got a band for ya. Don't pay him no mind. He always on some bullshit." He bluffed knowing Snatch was dead ass serious being his money was extra low now. Once they were back in the car, Castro screamed at Snatch for his stupidity. "Why would you do sum dumb shit like that?"

"I get it how I live...Big facts," he replied.

"I feel ya, but J.T. like family. He is the reason why we stay armed and dangerous," he informed Snatch.

"Oh, word," he replied.

"Big facts. Next week he gon' introduce me to his connect, so fall back. You know I gotcha."

Looking out the window, a thick white woman in spandex with long blond hair caught Snatch's attention as she was crossing the street. "Damn, shorty thicker than a bowl of oatmeal," he shouted amiss. "Looking at her is like teasing a hungry man with a steak."

"Facts. She is a whole lot of woman to be white, with a truck load of sex appeal," Castro said, lusting behind the wheel. "She definitely can get it." They continued in conversation about women while Rick Ross blasted as they entered Durham city limits. "Bruh, look in the glove compartment and grab that box of blunts," Castro said, blending into traffic.

Snatch lit the blunt, took a few pulls and passed it to Castro. He coughed, hitting his chest like King Kong. "That's gas."

Castro reached for the blunt laughing at his comrade who'd had a rough upbringing after his father died by the hands of some Jamaicans he extorted from time to time. Devastated from the tragedy he turned treacherous and began a life of crime filling the void with what he thought was the greatest sense of satisfaction as well as his first business opportunity. His mind was twisted.

"Bruh, drop me off at my B.M. crib. I need to go spend some time with my son. Shit, I been getting to the money for like a month now, and ain't got shit to show for it," Snatch said as reality of his situation set in. "Shit's got to change. I been spending reckless as fuck. It's time we go hard, my nigga."

"Bruh, you just now realized that shit? Don't get me wrong, you be getting to the bag, but you never got shit to show for it. You see, I stay in the trap, but I stack my bread as well. Don't worry though. Shit 'bout to get better for all of us. Jade is working on a major play right now. I can't call it right now, but she has been spending a lot of quality time with Malik. The last I heard, she 'bout to carry the team into the playoffs, and you know how we do once on the big stage."

"Yeah, but this time around I'm trying to win it all...I can't believe we slipped like that...I need a mil to myself."

"And you got the potential to get it...get focus, nigga," Castro said as he cruised through the inner streets of Durham, banging that 21 Savage.

"Bruh, where you headed?"

"To Central. Why?"

"I knew it. Drop me off, first. I ain't 'bout to sit in the car while you court that college cheerleader."

"Peep this shit out," Castro stated pulling alongside a cherry red Benz.

"Bruh, ain't that Fire's Range?"

"Yeah, and guess who he's fucking now?"

"Who, bruh?

"A.D."

"Bruh slipping for real with his shit parked out in front of A.D. crib like this."

"I think he moved in, 'cause the last few nights he's been crashing here."

"I thought she and Bunn got back together."

"Bruh, I thought Bunn just came home."

"That bitch ain't shit, yo."

"Shit, shorty gotta do what she has to do."

"Fuck that. That bitch ain't shit—"

"Okay, we got that established, but there's types of bitches...A bitch, hoe, and a slut."

"They all the same to me."

"I disagree. A bitch stay fly, get to the bag, holds her man down, but she gon' fuck around. A hoe is bisexual. She gon' straddle the fence because she lacks self-esteem and crave attention of a nigga and a bitch. She also get to the money but never has shit to show for it but the labels on her back. A slut will get you murdered, or locked the fuck up for the rest of your life if you ever get pussy-whipped," Castro said, dropping a jewel he had learned from Jade.

"So, you saying my B.M. a slut?"

"Nah, you said that."

"Nah, but everything you just said makes sense. My B.M. gots me passed fucked up. She ain't got shit and neither do I. But we always fly like we talk about it," Snatch said, inhaling the weed smoke.

The combination of reality, coinciding with the Za, given them both exceptional thoughts concerning their past, present and future, enhancing their mind to the basis of truth, when it comes to bitches. They both understood how they varied from one another. Both favored the "Bitch" conscious type because a bitch understands her man, the streets, the game, herself and the role she's supposed to play in life with a solid nigga.

"I heard she fucking that nigga Teflon."

"Fuck that bitch. That nigga Tef was at her crib when I called from the county."

"Did she ever come through and check ya?" Castro was curious to know if she came to visit him in the county.

"Come at me? The bitch barely accepted my calls. You know how she does when she gets on her bullshit," Snatch replied nonchalantly. "Come to think about it, that's probably who was at the house last night when I called. True story."

"She on some bullshit."

"Big facts! But she ain't gonna be satisfied til' she end up in a hearse."

Castro glanced over at Snatch noticing that he was off balance, yet serious at the same time. That was the second time this week that Snatch confessed his true feelings, and Castro knew he was a man of his word and would make his thoughts of killing her a reality. Thinking back to a past situation when he had to pull him off of her once, he decided to check his mental state further. "Let's cancel that bitch."

"Nah, I would never do that. She got my son, bruh."

"Well, end of conversation," Castro said, wanting to change the topic. "Yo, did you ever get that from Hysheem?"

"Yeah, I got it...and he moved all dem shits. Bruh solid. I fucks with bruh. But check this shit out. I was over on Instead the other night and I saw him jump out of a midnight Camero. They say he moving that boy now for Malik."

"Keep a close eye on that nigga, 'cause whatever he got going on, is stashed in his grandma crib."

"On it."

"I toldcha', it's only a matter of time before the streets is ours."

"I receive that. But have you noticed a difference in how Jade been moving lately?" Snatch asked suspiciously.

"More less... but it's all for the good, trust me. Quiet as kept, she tryna have a hundred mil before she twenty-eight. She got vision, bruh. You should build with her some time, homie."

"You think Malik fucked her yet?"

"I'm trying to get money, I ain't got time to worry about what they got going on. But if he did, it cost 'em a few stacks."

"Shit, I heard the nigga Face dumped a duffle bag full of money on the bed for the pussy." Snatch spoke as though he knew the facts. "Then she snatched like a chicken from his grip and made it look like somebody from his line of shooters did it."

They both burst out laughing thinking about the extremely attractive woman who bathed in the tears of her clients-slash-lovers and how she anointed herself with the blood of her victims. However, only those within her circle knew the ultimate. The personality outsiders would never imagine.

Chapter 5

Ceelo pushed his M6 coupe through the outskirts of Durham and rounded the corner of Ellis Road just blocks away from Jade's condo. He'd tried to call her to inform her of his whereabouts and to tell her to be ready, but he didn't get an answer. He considered texting her, but time was of the essence and he didn't want to keep his connect waiting.

As he got closer to his destination, thoughts of what she may be wearing entered his mind. Jade knew just how to market her confidants...by making herself the star attraction. Crushing the other women he's dated, she was a major distraction to him, which was very odd to him. Every time he saw her, it felt like July Fourth. She had this same effect if not more on all who stood in her presence for the first time.

Ceelo slowed and came to a stop in front of Jade's condo. Gazing at the organic elements defining her expensive taste, he wondered how she stayed stepping in designer labels and managed to pay her mortgage on time being she was unemployed. He pushed the thought from his mind and tapped softly on the horn, refocusing his attention to completing the task at hand.

Jade exited the condo, turned to set the alarm and walked gracefully towards the BMW as if she was walking down Paris runway with photographers trying to catch a TMZ moment. Her elegance commanded a second look. Dressed in an extremely salacious street brand found by Tyshineak's new clothing line, armed with luscious lips and killer cleavage, she smiled as she neared Ceelo's spaceship.

"Ma, you make that brand look famous," Ceelo complimented her as he stepped out of the suicide doors onto the pavement. "You got an ill ass shoe game," he said referring to the yellow Tyshineak Stewart heels she wore.

"That's because I ain't afraid to try new things...my swag, swags daily. I can rock whatever, whenever and my followers increase," she shot back as she slid into the driver's seat.

As Ceelo began walking around the coupe towards the passenger side she noticed he was dressed down in Gucci with the matching hat and sneakers, and a choke chain to enhance his demeanor.

"So, what brings you by today?" she stated as he slouched in the seat as the door descended, concealing their identities. "You must want something."

"Why you say that?"

"It's obvious. You only come around when you need me to do something for you. The last time I seen you, you left me lonely, playing with my pussy. What was that about?"

"If you would answer your phone, we wouldn't be having this conversation, but to answer your question about me leaving the room, well, some shit popped off that needed my undivided attention." There was a cautious frown on his face.

"Everything good?"

"I mean...I guess. It could have been much worse. Turn right here."

She made a right turn onto 15-501. "Can I make a stop real quick? I need to grab a second phone?"

"Nah, that shit gon' have to wait. I got a move to make."

"Alright, daddy. Can I go over fifty-five," she asked sarcastically.

"Look, when we pull up, I'ma need for you to stay in the car 'cause my peoples don't like doing business around new faces."

"So, why you bring me?"

"'Cause I give the orders. And besides, I enjoy your company."

"If you say so. But I need a deposit for the condo I've been looking at downtown."

"I can make that happen," Ceelo said, taking out his phone.

Out of nowhere, a seashell Porsche flew past them, going way over the speed limit, nearly swiping them off the road.

"What the fuck? Who was that?" Ceelo said paranoid. "Driving all crazy."

"Oh, that's Facts and 'em," Jade said feeling the chance to open up a new thought.

"Who? You talkin' 'bout Facts from Wall Town?" He was curious to know if he was the same Facts who robbed him for a chicken back in '08.

"Yeah, that's him. I heard he just hit some Mexicans for like a hundred and fifty bands."

"Woorrd," he stated with fire in his eyes.

"That's the word on the streets... They say he threw like twenty stacks in the strip club the other night. Fuck that nigga. They drugged my home girl up and raped her," she lied.

"For real?" Ceelo asked, wondering if by chance that could have happened to Joel.

As they pulled into the crowded parking lot of Target, Ceelo scanned the area as people moved to and from their vehicles. "Pull in right here." She pulled into the parking space next to a silver Maybach. "Wait here. I'll be right back." He climbed out the coupe, sliding into the backseat of the Maybach, slouching beside an unknown figure with the confidence of a Big Homie.

The man, known as Zulu, sat quietly watching BMF on a screen flushed inches under the headrest of the passenger seat. Standing at 6 '3", 310 pounds, dark skinned, bald headed, he was originally from Jamaica but was now a student at Duke University.

"Yea sta. Dead dem fucking boty boys bloodclotz. We hate dem fucking boty boys...who da broad star?" Zulu asked.

"That's the first lady...she's solid," Ceelo said, trying to prove a point.

"She's solid, ya tink?" Zulu smiled, showing off his diamond slugs in his mouth.

There was a moment of silence as both hustlers locked eyes, nodding at each other.

"We've been doing business what, like a year and a half now with no broad involvement?"

Ceelo nodded in agreement.

"Why broad now?" Zulu relit the blunt. Zulu then shut off the plasma and shifted around to face Ceelo. He reached between his legs and retrieved a Target shopping bag and handed it to Ceelo. "You tink you can handle dis?"

Ceelo observed the bag's contents and stared at Zulu somewhat shocked. So shocked he did a double take into the bag. He saw several kilos more than he normally got on consignment. "No doubt...What's the ticket on dis chicken?" Ceelo asked, closing the deal while eyeing the semiautomatic weapon beside Zulu.

A moment of silence settled as he sparked a second blunt to life. "Sixty-five," he said smoothly. "Dats 85% pure dope..." His thick accent evoked. "Dat, you can put a seven on one if you like. Dats good stuff I give you. I came all the way from Corsica by way of my family in Monte Carlo. Dey got much love for me," Zulu said, pounding his chest with his fist. "You owe me a big favor for the low price. Big favor, big favor."

"Big Facts...Anything you need, I gotcha."

"Okay. Me gon' hold you to dat." He hit the blunt once more. "Beware da woman," he warned suddenly.

"Who Jade?" Ceelo asked, puzzled.

"You'll soon see...she appears to be what you tink you need, but in time you will see her dark side. If you ain't tryna to hear me, don't," he warned as he flicked the plasma back on.

Ceelo exited the Mercedes Benz and slid back into the M6 with Jade.

"Damn, who was in there smoking? A gang of Jamaicans? All that damn smoke," Jade asked as Ceelo entered the coupe, setting the bag on the back seat.

"Don't worry 'bout that, just pull off." He responded by looking around.

Two hours later at the stash house, Jade sat on the plush L-shaped sofa with her back again at the pillows, legs crossed, sipping a glass of Patron while Ceelo stood on the patio smoking on some pressure. He then stepped back inside, reached for the phone that sat on its charger on the table and dialed a series of numbers.

"Hello?" Destiny answered.

"How you miss being independent... Where your home girl at?" He asked.

"She in the back, on the net ordering some books," She stated all ghetto like.

"That's what up. So, what's been good with you?"

"Oh, not much. Just studying for my exams next week."

"Don't study too hard," he said thinking he heard a clicking noise in the background as if her phone was tapped. "What's that clicking sound?"

"Ain't no telling with these phones today." She explained in a sexy tone. "So, what you and Joel 'bout to get into?"

"We were going to look at some houses, but I got something to handle."

"Like what?" She asked curiously.

"I need you to come through and step on a few spider webs for me." He informed her in code.

"No problem. Just let me know when I need to pull up."

"I need you to pull up like right now, real talk—"

"Here come Joel now," she stated cutting him off.

"Hey, baby," Joel said.

"Hello beautiful."

"What are you doing? We still going shopping today?"

"Yeah, I gotcha, but I got something to handle right now."

"That's all you ever say," she said sarcastically. "When it's time to be with me?"

"Don't do that."

"Boy, bye. Anyway, guess what?"

"What?"

"We got the house in Cary. I have to go back out there tomorrow to meet the furniture company so they can deliver the furniture."

"What did you do with the other shit?"

"I gave most of it to my sister. She just moved into her new apartment."

"Oh, aiight." He overheard Destiny tell Joel she was about to leave.

"So, are you coming over later, baby?"

"I can't say for such right now, 'cause I got so much shit to do. Just hit me when you get the house situated," he said tired of talking.

"Wait for it," she said, rudely hanging up on him.

He stared at the phone as if she could see him. "I know this bitch didn't just hang up on me." He whispered mad as a man who just blew a trial. He then walked in the kitchen and stood over Jade as she sat stacking the kilos of heroin on the table.

She glanced up at him noticing that his whole demeanor had changed completely like a coin had been flipped from heads to tails. "Something wrong, daddy?"

"Nah, I'm good," he stated moodily. He wanted to share what had been really bothering him, but nothing would come out.

Jade knew that something troubled him, so she stood and walked around the table to where he was standing, breaking the silence by snapping the rubber glove she wore loudly. She then leaned over and hugged him, resting her chin upon his head, not liking to see him upset; wishing he would converse with her about whatever was bothering him because his spirits seemed very low. "Something's bothering you." She inched her hands under his shirt, rubbing his chest, inspiring him to open.

"I need a favor."

"If it's about getting to the bag, I'm wit it," she said seriously.

"That seems to be the only thing that moves you."

"Facts! I gotta get it how I live."

"I need someone dependable to help me move this work." He pointed to the product.

"What about Trigger and Lucky?" She asked suspicious because it's never been a problem for them to move the work.

"Did you hear anything I just said? I need dependable people. Dem my niggas but they hot right now," Ceelo said, rubbing his head.

"How they hot and they ain't even been down here a month yet?" Jade asked, confused.

"Dem niggas beefing right now wit sum niggas outta Raleigh. I ain't got room for that shit. I'm tryna move dis work."

"That's understood, but I assumed they were doing they thing."

"Yeah, they getting the job done, but like I said, they too risky right now. I honestly want dem niggas to lay low for a minute," he said, shaking his head.

"So, you need some niggas to move dis work?"

"Basically, but not niggas I gotta run down for my money. I need another spot other than the Mac that's banging."

Jade walked around the table, contemplating on what was said, although she knew he wasn't a killer, any confrontation could force his hand and make him one out of fear. Jade considered her comrades for a second knowing they all qualified to move the work, however, she felt Malik would be the best candidate to work under Ceelo because he could be trusted. "I got someone in mind...this young kid from my hood. He gets to the bag, his mind right, he is loyal, but he still in school. He wants to be able to work the trap all day," she explained, trying to come up with a way to work around his schedule.

"We can work around that," he said after thinking on what Jade had brought to the table. "Just holla at 'em and let me know what's good."

"What's in it for me?"

"Just introduce us and I gotcha. He better be built like that."

"Oh, this lil nigga really get to the bag," she whispered seductively, wrapping her arms around his waist.

"Good. Let's get it."

They began kissing passionately with thoughts of a quickie before anyone else arrived.

He slowly unbuttoned her blouse, exposing her firm breasts confined within her Dior bra. Breathing inwardly through clenched teeth she moaned softly as he smothered her mouth with his tongue between her lips. She met his tongue with hers as she fumbled with his Fendi belt buckle, desperately trying to free his bulging monster from his jeans, when suddenly a loud knock sounded at the door. They quickly regrouped and examined one another.

"Get the door, crazy. You good?" She laughed.

"Who is it?"

"It's me. Destiny," the child-like voice said as if it belonged to a fifteen year old school girl.

Ceelo unlocked and opened the door and stared at the angel that stood before him. Destiny Damina Cortez was extravagant in her six-foot-frame. Her curvaceous new body was an attention magnet complimented by her brown eyes and long blonde hair accenting her flawless baby doll face, and caramel skin tone. An exotic combination of Mexican and black, she had a provocative stance and induced sensual feelings in all who gazed upon her beauty when entering their presence. Dressed in a Valentine Red Dior top and jeans that looked as if they had been sprayed on her, with matching red and cream Christian Louboutin stilettos. "You possess a natural beauty and elegance rarely seen," he said as she stepped through the door.

As she made her way through the living room into the kitchen, she felt envy seeping from Jade, a woman she'd never met. Their casual glance told both exotic roses all they needed to know. "Hello, I'm Destiny," she said, extending her hand to Jade. "And you are?"

Jade was in awe of her beauty and directness instantly. "Jade, nice to meet you," she responded.

After the introductions were over, they decided to get to the business at hand. Six hours later, after working through a stressful situation as though they were master chemists, they broke down each kilo into grams before departing with five bands that Ceelo had paid them equally for their assistance. There was more money to be made and Jade and Ceelo were out to get to it, or die trying.

Chapter 6

After an intense practice, Malik hit the shower, quickly washed, dressed and made his way through the crowded lock room filled with members of his team to a full-size mirror and examined himself. Dressed in a navy blue and teal DKNY leather jacket, matching long sleeve shirt with the blue and white DKNY logo highlighting his dark blue jeans and Sprite colored Air Force Ones, he exemplified a well-dressed, ultra fly hustler. Standing six feet tall with wavy hair and unshakable confidence, he knew he was dripped, and niggas would hate.

As he joined the crowded atmosphere of students lingering in the hallways, he noticed an exotic rose among adequate flowers fumbling with her locker. He slowly crept from behind, placing his arms around her waist, pulling her firmly against his body while admiring her Caeser hairdo. "Excuse me, miss, there is something I would like to say to you respectfully. You're more beautiful than all the flowers growing on this earth. You got a man?" He whispered.

Recognizing his voice, she giggled. "Stop playing, Malik, I'm already late for class," she responded, pressing back against his love muscle, teasing him.

"Well, at least let me walk you to class so these thots will stop stalking me."

"Boy, bye," she whispered softly, spinning to face him. "How was practice?" she asked, looking into his eyes.

He looked her over lustfully, feeling a wave of heat throughout his body.

Asia stood 5'9" with a taffy-colored skin tone with almond eyes accenting her full juicy lips. She was dressed in a pair of Moschino jeans that fit perfectly for her legs and body shape with Christian Louboutin heels and bag. The Moschino shirt she wore enhanced the swollen breast that never failed to mesmerize him. She had a strong personality defined by an urge for sex that created her persona, being the only child of middle-class parents. An underage adult attending high school weathering the storms of the world as she attempted to conquer her dreams of becoming an attorney. She and Malik met during the first week of high school, when he accidentally bumped into her.

"Malik." She called him a second time.

"Huh?"

"I know you heard me. How was practice?"

"Like any other practice, I guess. How was your day?"

"Loneliness has been my constant companion all week. I really missed you. You miss me?"

"Like a king whose queen has gone away to stay." He responded by kissing her, showering her with affection.

Smelling the fresh fragrance of aroma about his neck she stepped back, admiring him with a sensual look in her eyes. "Where you off too now?" she asked, placing her hands on her hips.

He looked at her, noticing the insecurity in her voice and demeanor. "To a party later."

"Where?" she asked bluntly.

"At The Center."

"The Center? What center?" she asked, perplexed.

"The center of dem thighs of yours," he responded, looking down in that direction.

They exploded in laughter.

"You so nasty." She giggled. "What if I don't let you in?"

Malik burst out laughing again and suddenly stopped. "Then I will just sneak through the back door."

"No, the hell you ain't. Your crazy ass."

"I'm only crazy about you," he said as she reached in her locker, removing her Moschino jacket. "Close your eyes, I got something special for you." He extracted a jewelry box from his Louis Vuitton bag, handing it to her. "You can open them now."

"What is it?" she asked, holding it as if it was going to explode. "Ooh! This for me?" She removed the mystical diamond encrusted Bentley key swinging on a diamond chain. Tears began to weld up in her eyes. "How many carats is it?"

"Fifty. Why you crying?" He wiped her tears.

"Because it's beautiful, Malik," she replied softly as if she was speechless, like she saw Jesus in the physical.

"But, not as beautiful as you, Asia. You're my diamond," he whispered, placing the flashy jewelry around her neck.

"Baby, this chain cost at least forty bands. Where you getting all this money from lately?" she asked, knowing the answer.

He eyed her as she dropped her head, and he gently raised it with his finger. "Don't ever question me."

She was about to give him a piece of her mind, but she decided otherwise by the gesture of his affection. "You right...just be careful, daddy," she said, thumbing the Bentley key, caressing its ice.

"I'll take that into consideration."

"I love you, Malik."

"I love you more."

She blushed and kissed his lips. "So, what time you coming to the Center? I might even let you through the back door just once. That's totally VIP and no man has ever entered my juicy apple hole."

"Until now." He unbuckled his belt. "We can get it in right here, if you like."

"Boy, bye. You too much." She giggled.

"Look who's talking...you're the nympho."

"That I am and more," she said seductively in her soft, sensual voice.

They kissed and embraced one another before going their separate ways with high expectations of fulfilling each other's desires at a later time. He marveled at how spectacular her ass looked as she sashayed down the hallway. *I'ma bless that ass tonight,* he thought.

***

Jade sat outside the school in the parking lot of Hillside High as she checked the time on her platinum Aqua Master watch wondering where Malik was, knowing practice ended twenty minutes ago. She glanced over to see a 911 Porsche. She smiled at Castro who was reclined behind the wheel, nodding to Meek Mill while smoking a blunt full of broccoli with Snatch. Scrutinizing the crowd of high schoolers, she blew the horn of her rented SUV, attracting Malik's attention, motioning with her hand to call him over. Her instinct gave her an unusual desire.

As he approached both cars, Castro and Snatch exited theirs. "Red Rum Salute." Snatch said, saluting Malik. "What's good, homie?"

"New day, new opportunity, ya dig," Malik replied. "What's good wit you two?"

"Getting money and fucking bitches; you know how we do," Castro said, pulling on the oversized blunt.

"Get it how you live," Malik said, giving both felons dap.

Unexpectedly a young chick with a Porsche body dressed snugly in some sea-blue jeans, a blue and white long sleeve shirt that read "Welcome To Durham" and some blue and white Retro Jordan's walked by the three hustlers. They all looked down at the ridiculous fatty that sat tauntingly on her back, as her seductive walk fascinated them all.

"Bruh, who dat?" Snatch asked Malik.

"Oh, that's Kimberly."

"She's a trophy by all means necessary. I'm 'bout to go holla at dat," Snatch said as he stormed off to meet the young diva who had inspired him in countless ways.

"Yo, bruh a fool. What you 'bout to get into homie?" Malik asked.

"I'm 'bout to slide by Peggy's crib," Castro said.

"No, you 'bout to spend some money," Malik said as Jade lowered her window.

"Malik, come ride with me, I need to holla at you," Jade said.

Castro jumped in his car as Snatch continued to spit game that was too difficult for her to resist.

"Whatcha got for me? Another client or what?" Malik asked, leaning in the driver side window.

"Actually, no and yes. I'm still working on a potential client, but another situation just fell in my lap that may benefit all of us."

"Elaborate."

"Remember the nigga Ceelo, right? Well, he's been watching you like a hawk, and say every time he comes through you in the trap moving grams like it's Black Friday," she stated, as she delivered some powerful remarks about Malik's involvement in the streets.

"I'm just trying to run dis cake up. A lot of niggas getting to the bag, but it's different when you start from zero."

"Big facts."

"If he ain't talking at least three byrd's or better, we ain't speaking," he said, keeping the conversation exclusive like his dress code. "I gotta huge responsibility. I gotta feed my hood, so if he ain't talking my lingo, I don't mind going up and down the interstate to make shit happen."

"We can get that and more, as long as we got the clientele to move it."

"On consignment?" He asked, receiving a nod in affirmation. "I don't want it that way. I'd rather pay for mine," he added firmly.

"I agree, but we can use this opportunity to our advantage." Her words motivated him.

"More less… I can see where you going with this."

Before she could utter another word, Snatch walked up beaming with personal affections too difficult to hide.

"Bruh, you got more games than a deck of cards," Malik said, unamazed his comrade had bagged Kimberly, 'cause he had crazy potential to accomplish anything he wanted.

"Facts. I'm 'bout to give up my thot for this bitch."

"Boy, bye. Ain't nobody trying to hear that shit. You the only thot I see!" Jade yelled.

"Close your ears then," Snatch shot back.

"That's why you ain't got no money now. Always tricking on dem bitches!"

"Look who's talking. You hating 'cause a fly nigga like me ain't threw a few stacks your way."

"Nigga, please. Don't even go there. This pussy is bullet proof. You couldn't shoot your shot if you had Jay-Z money."

Malik and Castro busted out laughing.

"Bruh, don't let her clown you like that," Castro said between laughter.

"I still love you, boo," Jade said in a flirty way.

"I love you too, ma," Snatch said as he and Castro climbed in the coupe.

"Bruh, you riding wit us or what?"

"Nah, I'm riding with Jade. We 'bout to make a play. I'll catch up with y'all niggas later."

Castro looked at Snatch and started laughing again.

"Oh, you think dat shit was funny?" Snatch said, feeling defeated.

"You better leave shorty alone," Castro said pulling off, listening to Young Thug's newest music.

Moments later, Malik jumped in Jade's SUV and she pulled off, blending into the evening traffic.

"Why did you come to me about working for dude?" Malik asked as Cardi B blasted through the speakers.

"Because I trust you, and besides, I like the way you move, and I know you will take advantage of this opportunity and make something of it," she said as she dipped in and out of traffic. "And I'm looking forward to that Bentley you promised me."

"I thought you didn't want me in the streets?"

"I don't, but I feel like you can handle it as long as I'm around to assist you," she said feeling good about the choice she had made of recruiting Malik.

"I'm in. Whatever it takes for us to get to a hundred-mil...let's get to it."

"We will get there. Just do what you gotta do to infiltrate his circle, 'cause once you're in, we all win."

"Say less. I'ma play this nigga close like Baby did Lil Wayne."

"You ever heard the name Zulu?" She asked, wondering if he ever heard the name on the streets.

"Zulu? Not off hand. Why? Our target?"

"Not sure yet. All I know is he drives a Maybach and he may be Ceelo's connection."

"And how do you know all of this?"

"'Cause I drove Ceelo over to meet him."

"So you think Ceelo working for Zulu?"

"That's what I know. That's why you must play your cards right in order for us to see this opportunity all the way through."

"Consider it done."

"One last thing. Castro and Snatch must not know what we have going on," she warned.

"But—"

"But nothing, Malik. I know we are a team but everything ain't for everybody. As long as niggas eating, they don't need to know where the food is coming from. You understand me?"

"You already..." he said as Jade pulled up in front of Asia's house. Before exiting the SUV, he leaned over and gave her a friendly peck on the cheek.

Jade's eyes widened, shocked by his gesture of affection. Her heart fluttered; she thought he was about to kiss her on the lips.

Chapter 7

Ceelo called Joel from the stash house and told her to meet him at South Point Mall. He then followed her to their new luxurious estate which sat nestled only miles from Raleigh Durham International Airport in an exclusive area in Cary.

"Queen Elizabeth's already made their delivery," Joel said, seeing the plush wicker sofa, stacked with hand embroidered cushions as they entered the angled entry which opened to the gallery-style foyer with views that extend through the core of the home.

Joel always had an eye for fashion. She had purchased two black granite end tables and matching coffee tables that sat on a black and beige carpet which covered the entire living room. A 72" fish tank stocked with colorful beige and black rocks and a nine tropical fish swarm complimented the lavish decor.

"This shit is crazy, baby...You decorated all this by yourself?" Ceelo asked, dropping onto the sofa, admiring the marble fireplace with its ornamental iron screen. He glanced over at the 75-inch plasma TV flushed within the wall above the fireplace, which was lined with family photos. "I'm loving the surround system...Big Facts."

"You really like it?" she asked, smiling like a Colgate advertisement.

"Of course. Come here," he said gazing into her eyes. He pulled her towards him.

"Baby, it's only right that I see to it that you are comfortable. You mean the world to me," she said, kissing him as she grabbed his hand. "Come on, let me show you the kitchen." She smiled, pulling him.

"I'm right behind you," he said as they entered the beautiful kitchen designed to serve a variety of occasions as well as easy, everyday meals.

A black walk around stove with a marble top, two built in refrigerators sat in front for easy access and entry, European paneled cabinetry with sleek, stainless-steel appliances and maple-plank hardwood floors.

"Now, I can cook without being cramped up," she said as she dragged her finger across the granite top.

His phone sounded, letting him know that one of his workers were in need of more work. He removed his phone from his cargo pocket, speaking briefly for a few moments. Joel showed him the rest of the estate, upstairs, the bathrooms, rear balcony and the winding staircase that led down to the pool and spa area.

"So, are you ready for the main event?" she asked, stopping inches from the master bedroom.

"I'm always ready for the bedroom."

She opened the door slowly and stepped inside. Ceelo was awed by the burgundy oakwood sleigh bed, matching chest, dresser, and nightstands with lush carpeting. He was excited and admonished her good taste.

"You wanna go for a ride?" He teased her. "And put a few miles on it?"

"Let's wait awhile. We just got here."

"So, what's the main event?"

"This," she said, opening her trench fur coat.

Ceelo's eyes widened larger than fifty-cent pieces. "Oh my god," he said through clenched teeth.

Joel stood holding her fur coat wide open, exposing her bralette and skirted thong. "This is all yours, baby," she whispered, walking over to the bed. "Do whatever you like."

Her fur coat dropped to the floor before she gently lay back, parting her legs.

Ceelo stared at the swollen mound of her secret opening, licking his lips.

"Cum have your way, daddy," she said, motioning with her finger.

He quickly climbed in bed, lying beside her.

"Mmm...Mmm..." She teased, rubbing his hairy chest.

He lay on his side, propping up on his elbow and began caressing the full length of her body, while her black, curly hair lay across the pillow, highlighting her flawless pecan skin tone. "Why you staring at me like that?" he asked caressing her full-size lips and looking into her dreamy eyes.

After three years together she was amazed at how strong their relationship had blossomed since their first encounter. He had always been there for her since day one with an understanding heart, an open mind, and for that reason she showed him unconditional love. She could seek his help in any matter. To her that meant a lot in a relationship. Not once had she ever known him cheat with other women, knowing this made her very emotional.

"I'm good, but I can tell something is bothering you."

"Really, it's nothing."

"Don't tell me it's nothing when I know when something is bothering you," he said staring at her.

She inhaled, her firm breasts swelling, then exhaled. "I just wish you didn't have to go tonight. We never spend much time together any more...please stay the night," she begged with tears filling her eyes.

"Baby, don't do this. Not tonight. You know I gotta take this trip. I won't be gone long. Only for like a day or two, then it's me and you. Facts."

"You always say that, but as soon as you get back, it's always something else. You don't know what you wanna do. One minute you say this is your last run, then the next minute you at the stash spot doing whatever you do. I wish you would make up your mind before someone does it for you."

"What the fuck that supposed to mean? You know something I don't?"

"I know the only way out is jail or death. I love you, Ceelo, and I would hate to see you throw your life away like that."

"But I do it for us."

"Well, from what I counted last night, I think we good. We have more than enough to invest in what we discuss. I just wish you would walk away while you're ahead." She challenged him.

"I don't have any problem with that after this last run. I promise you, if you just bear with me for six more months we gon' be set for life, for real."

"So, six more months and we good? If you say so. I guess I have no choice but wait it out if it's gon' be like that," she said, pulling him to her. "I love you so fucking much. Fuck me before you go." She expressed it with passion. A strong, wonderful feeling burned inside her. She desperately wanted to feel him inside.

He passionately kissed her lips as they entwined. She raised her hips into the hard erection swollen inside her. Shivers shot through her body as the intense pleasure was slowly taking her breath away. She began breathing harder until suddenly she climaxed and nothing else mattered but his blissful kiss.

Unaware of his hand sliding down the length of her body, she panted as she felt him reach her stomach. He eventually found his way to the underside of her breast. The moment he cupped them, sharp sensations of pleasure traveled through her body, arousing her desire even more. He removed her bralette, tossing it to the floor, and began caressing her stiff, erect nipples.

"Please...Oh God...Pl...Please, baby...put it back in me...suck 'em hard...Owww..." She panted in a soft whisper as he sucked her nipples, driving her completely crazy. She reached down and grabbed his lion-sized cock and slipped it back inside her, feeling the swollen head part her lips.

"Damn, you got that water," he said pulling out.

"Fuck me, daddy." She freaked when he slid his finger two inches up in her, working her juices, stimulating her mind as it reeled with unexpected passion surging through her with such a powerful sensation as though she was on fire. She gasped loudly as his lips sucked on her erect eraser-size nipples, setting off sensations of intoxicating pleasure. "Yes...Yes...that's my spot." She gasped between breaths.

He started caressing her as she sucked hard on her breasts, running his hands up and down her body. Her imagination heightened as he assaulted her swollen lips wildly with his middle finger through her hot, wet pussy, until he felt slippery secretions on his hand.

Joel was dripping from all the excitement. In fact so wet that making love was no longer a part of the equation. She wanted him to fuck her hard, long and deep, like he would a slut.

As he continued to finger-fuck her, her whole body trembled and her lungs were about to explode. "Ahhh..." She cried. "Damn, this feels so good." She inhaled, grinding her hips up to meet his thrusting finger, unable to stand the foreplay any longer.

He looked into her eyes. However, they were closed. Wondering why, he suddenly stopped. The moment she opened her eyes he reached down and literally ripped her thin thong off.

She was astonishingly turned on by his aggressiveness, as he braced himself above her and reached down, grabbing his enormously large love muscle, sliding it smoothly up and down the slit of her pussy as she became more wet. He then easily slid it in through her slippery secretions. Stroking her relentlessly, bringing her to the brink as she moaned, feeling him deep up inside her.

"Oh God...yes...yess...yesssss...cum in my daddy... ohhh...yessssss!" She panted from the smacking sounds bubbling from between her legs. Slowly she raised her legs high as her body took over, using her heels to rotate her hips in circular motions as she met each thrust. "Oooohhh..."

In the heat of passion her emotions took over, as he ruggedly pounded in and out of her. He could feel the wetness seeping out with every push forward, ramming his stiffness, and forcing a deep moan from her sensual lips, as her liquid smeared upon him.

She cried out in desire, wanting to reach its completion as her body began trembling and felt it no longer belonged to her, and he was master of her mind as he banged her back out. She continued grinding with his strokes to reach her orgasm.

"Ohhh...I'm... mm...mm...m...uhhh..." She cried loudly, making sexual noises as her legs spread wider. "Fuck!" She wanted more. She drew her legs back, pressing them against her breast, giving him total access. "C-C-Cummmmmming!" She screamed as her stomach muscle tightened. "Yesssss!"

She gave one last shudder. As her muscle contacted tightly around his love muscle he pulled out and rolled over on his back. She then performed oral sex on him until he was completely satisfied.

***

After showering, he jumped into his Range Rover and drove to the Marriott to meet with Jade. He pulled into the back, flashed his lights twice, and another vehicle followed him as he parked out by the lake.

Jade pulled up alongside his Rover, killed the engine, and jumped into the Rover with Ceelo.

"Hi, daddy," she said, kissing him on the lips. "How you like the new place?"

"It's beautiful, Jade. It's nested in the cut like I always like. One of these days I'ma have to let you take a tour of it."

"A tour of it. It's that big?"

"Facts."

"You sure Joel won't mind?" She leaned her head on his shoulders.

He placed his arm around her smoothly. "You know I'm 'bout to be gone for a couple days, right? So, I need you to hold me down. See a few of my people, drop off some work here and there, and collect my money for me."

She lifted her head and stared into his eyes. "Where you going?" She asked, concerned. "You just got back from Alabama; can't it wait?"

"No, this has to be dealt with tonight."

"Can I come?"

"Not this time. Besides, I need you to hold me down."

"You on some bullshit. Where the fuck you going that you can't take me? I thought we were going shopping this weekend!" She screamed in anger.

"Girl, bye," he said, giving her a taste of her own medicine. "I'll be back before then."

"You got something for Malik?"

They conversed and reasoned with one another about business that he wanted her to attend to while he was away.

"You still haven't told me where you going," she added.

"Miami. Now do something to make me feel good." He tilted his seat back, shifting closer to her, slowly kissing her neck and lips.

She then whispered in his ear. "Oh, so you want some road head?" She moved her hand toward his crotch, fondling his dick through the fabric of his 1,000 jeans. She unzipped his pants slowly with intentions of making him hornier than ever. Freeing his swollen member she encircled it with her finger. "Mmmmmm... Damn, your dick feel like a steel pipe." She licked the mushroom-sized head of his banana-sized cock. "You wanna cum in my mouth, don't you?" She asked as she licked up and down the shaft of his dick, while feeling his pulse beat through his erect penis. She anticipated how long before he would burst in her mouth, feeling his hardness against the back of her throat. She moved slowly with her lips over his head as she worked him back and forth with her hand.

A groan of burning desire escaped his mouth from the sensation of her tongue sliding through his pee hole, as the gap in her mouth turned the tricks. He couldn't believe the pleasure and delight she drew from his inner existence sucking him inside out. He ran his fingers through her hair and around her neck as she pleasured him in the most wonderful way. His body tingled with mind numbing pleasure from the intense contact, as he felt his muscle spasm from the frantic movement of her tongue running circles around the tip of his head. She then began sucking wildly, becoming excited, sliding her tongue against the thick veined organ as he was slamming the swollen head against the back of her tonsils, causing her to gag. As she clasped her lips tightly he began to move his hips upward, fucking her face. The wet sucking sounds caused him to mumble, "Damn, Jade, your head game is fire. Ooowww... Yeahhh." He moaned out loud.

Jade began bobbing her head faster, sucking his dick harder, wanting to make him cum so she could gulp it down, as she knew he would develop a massive explosion he would never forget. He caressed her large, firm breasts. He squeezed her nipple until she whimpered around his dick. As they became erect and hard he gently squeezed them, noticing how nice and wonderful they felt in his hands. Tiny rivulets of wetness built up in the crevice between her legs. She started sucking madly on his swollen gland, knowing she was now ready for his cum to run down her throat. As she felt his rod contract, she knew he was nearing to spit.

He arched up, thrusting his dick further into the suction of her hot, wet lips, gasping loudly.

"Fuck...Ohh...Damn...shit!" He closed his eyes as his hips began jerking wildly as his dick swelled in size.

Sperm rushed into her mouth with a powerful force exploding against the back of her throat.

As she swallowed his cum in long gulps, the ecstasy was greater than what Joel had given him. She slowly removed her mouth from his dick and wiped him clean, zipping him back up as they both breathed with exhausted gasps cherishing the moment.

They talked and came to an agreement. He then reached into the glove compartment and pulled out a wad of about $5,000 and handed it to her, along with a Nike duffle bag he had retrieved from the back seat of his Range Rover. They then said their goodbyes, driving off as silently as they came.

Ceelo drove in silence with his thoughts and deep in his feelings trying to figure out how and why he allowed himself to leave Jade with the responsibility of moving two kilos of heroin, knowing he was taking a risk. However, he loved her in so many ways, and with that love came a level of trust. He felt guilty about lying to Joel and Jade as far as his whereabouts for the next couple of days, although he sensed Jade knew he was lying about going to Miami, because he had already re-upped. However, he hoped she'd understand if she ever found out he had lied to her because she was a good friend and he didn't want anything to ruin their companionship, which was open and honest.

He tapped the horn lightly as he pulled behind a black sapphire metallic Aston Martin. Seconds later an exotic rose in her early twenties with an angelic face and long beautiful hair stepped from being the wheel of the Vanquish.

She was tall and curvaceous with a treacherous demeanor and new body. Her eyes glittered under the moonlit sky, highlighting her Egyptian bronze skin with a radiant allure. She was thoroughly dressed in a blue business suit with a button-down shirt underneath her jacket as though she was coming from work.

"Hey beautiful," he said as he stepped out of the Range Rover. "You been waiting long?" He asked before kissing her on the lips.

"Not too long. Probably 'bout five minutes if that," she said unlocking the truck. "Can you be so kind and grab my bags for me? I'll drive us to the airport 'cause you look drained," she said unaware of how true that statement really was.

"Damn, we're only gonna be gone for a week. Why you pack so much shit?" He asked her.

"Obviously, you don't have the slightest idea when it comes to people in Quebec. There's no telling what might go down in a moment's notice. They party harder than we do...you'll see. That's why I made sure I packed as many outfits as needed."

"Girl, bye. When I finish with you, partying will be the last thing on your mind," Ceelo said, tossing her Louis Vuitton luggage in the Jeep, slamming the door shut.

She took her cell phone out of her Fendi bag and placed a call to her employer. After the call, she placed her cell back into her bag and noticed she was still wearing her shoulder holster which concealed a .45. She then unhooked the holster and placed the gun in the glove compartment, knowing her coworker would pick up the company car later.

"I know you wasn't just talking to who I think you were talking to," he asked as she climbed into the Range.

"Boy, bye. I would never do that. She would kill both of us if she found out."

"So, who were you whispering to, then?"

"My mother. I told her we were heading to the airport. They—" She paused, realizing she was sharing too much information. "My parents are very overprotective. I don't want them worrying and have every federal agent in America looking for us. That wouldn't be a smart choice, now would it?" She asked, pulling off into traffic.

In minutes Ceelo was asleep with a smile on his face. Jade had done her job with perfection.

Chapter 8

Four body counts and six shootouts later, Malik and his comrades sat in a nested condo on the outskirts of Durham, discussing their choices with two million in cash, while lavishly smoking blunts and drinking gold bottles as if they were Sunkist sodas.

Within four months Ceelo had promoted Malik and had given him major responsibilities; molding and creating himself into a legend beyond his counterparts. Towering above those in notoriety working hard through stressful days and long nights, Malik had grown to love the game with a passion. Nothing had given him more motivation than the love of the streets, money, and its power.

The operation had become more of a corporation than a drug outfit, where he learned a loyalist didn't compromise with his own rules, so he stuck to his game plan. However, he often rationalized things before blowing a fuse or his prospective gain in money. His individuality changed as he grew in every aspect although his foes never lived to advertise anything if they violated in any way because he would crush them, their shooter's and empire if he needed to. With nothing more than a diploma fresh out of high school he was skillful with leadership and also mastered metric weight; not to mention how to cut and prepare heroin extremely well. His vision of profiling and analyzing others' psychological behavior had sharpened, allowing him to spot undercover agents, stick up wolves and plain old vultures trying to feed off the dead while they were still walking.

Jade, Snatch, and Castro always surrounded him with loyalty and respect, never acting like soldiers or the help running errands for rank. They knew he was the big homie even though he wasn't the oldest.

During a brawl one night at a club in Charlotte, Snatch buck fifty a dude and got arrested. He was arrested again for punching a store clerk in the face for shortchanging him. Once his parole officer got word, he threatened to violate him and send him back to prison. However, that day never came, as Jade followed him one night as he left the strip club, splattering his brains with a .44 Magnum hollow point slug.

Snatch was released from custody due to the fact that his parole officer never got a chance to file the paperwork; just the luck of the hand. Malik, Snatch and Castro knew it was Jade that had such a sensitive matter with anyone. She strongly took to heart the silence as a code of the streets and believed in it fully. Loyalty was a soldier's last breath was the motto and led to the murder of a dude who tried to rob Malik one night. Jade killed all chances of a Machiavelli retaliation hit to be put on Malik. A killer only she knew about.

Castro, who had grown smarter himself, advised a color-coded system for the bundles they sold for $10 a bag at a rapid speed. Their hustle made the characters into the movie *Paid in Full* look like stick figures trying to sell cement blocks as weight.

All the dope boys in Durham tried to follow his color-coded system thinking it would generate large sums of money, however, the color played a small role in how quickly his team took over the city. Leading to the death of wannabe, Mr. Tough Guy pushing his product disguised in bags resembling theirs, Snatch killed the dude in broad daylight, sending an instant message forcing everyone to call out colors and names of the product they were seeking in the hood.

Due to the mesmerized power and respect of Malik, Jade, Castro, and Snatch only dealt in grams and collected large sums of money from The Mac, Wall Town, Fayetteville Street Projects, South Side, and the West End. On average they grossed around one million a week from the sales. However, a percentage went to Ceelo, and they divided the rest between themselves and their individual shooters and distribution team. They were quickly moving up in the game, prospering as their name rung throughout every hood in Durham like a church bell.

Malik and his shooters were on demon time when out of town hustlers tried to move their product in Durham, often relieving them of their jewels if they had Malik's permission. No one was allowed to dig in their pockets otherwise. Malik and his felons were moving up the ladder to Big Meech status. Ceelo kept Malik under his umbrella as he planned to do one last shipment and the last brick he would toss at the penitentiary.

"Bruh, this Patron got my dick in the dirt," Snatch said, slumped over the marble countertop. "We been counting dis money all-fucking-day. How much more money you gon' pull out the stash? We did dis type money just out of Henderson," he asked as he glanced down at his designer wristwatch that read, 2AM.

"Big facts. That's like a second home to me." Jade spoke from a place of pureness.

They were all tired from counting as they finally completed the task.

Malik had his eyes on them like a hawk, smiling with personal thoughts on way to make his vision a tangible reality. "Look. It's a little too much in-house tension amongst us. I don't know what's going on between you demons but it needs to cease. We too fly to be on that indirect speaking. What we have established within our circle and accomplished in the streets was built on a level of solid love we have for one another. The love we reflect amongst ourselves, is reflected back to us through the love the hood show us on all levels. We the new leaders of the new school. We gon' be the first street billionaires. Our story will someday be told, so let's refresh the love we had for one another that we shared in the beginning. Whatever internal issue niggas got going on within us..." He pointed to each of his comrades. "Let it go...now. Today is a new day, a new opportunity to get rich with me, or allow your pride to destroy our foundation. What we say we birth.

"We are where we are today because of what we have been saying about ourselves, each other and our movement in the streets. When we pull up, the streets show the love we have for each other, because we family. We give life to what we say. That's why we must be mindful when we talk among ourselves 'bout each other. Because envy breeds hate. We a movement of love, passion, and motivation. We the Billionaire Boys who run with the undisputed queen of the city. We got too much hustle not to win." Malik spoke with mixed emotions, conviction, and love.

"Big facts," Jade started with big, big, energy.

"No cap, just look what you've drafted so far. In just weeks we went from jooking niggas to now calling the shots in Durham and Henderson," Malik stated, reflecting on the team's past.

"It's like I can't even pull up without a gang of infatuated women pulling up on sum. I need a Fendi bag full of money, just 'cause I'm slaying 'em," Castro threw out there so his team could see his side of the story. "If the pussy WAP, I don't mind gifting her for showing me a good time." He started receiving a new level of respect from his comrades.

Jade stood on her running Dior sneakers after swallowing the last of her drink. "But when niggas is getting real money, we need more than a bag full of money. We need estate money. We have to put in extra work because there's a shortage of men out here, so at times we have to share, especially when you're not as remarkable as me."

"More like we trapped by exchanging dope for dollars and the women mirror what we do, except for product in themselves," Malik asked, making sure he understood what she had said.

"Big facts. That's why I fucks with you, Big Homie. You be having me in space. It's like we one of the same with champagne dreams."

"Bruh, enough is enough. I'm tired and I know my bitch gon' wanna fuck when I touch that ass. I'm out," Castro said, sounding real sleepy.

Jade, Castro, Snatch, and Malik all stood on designer sneakers and wrapped themselves in their colorful mink coats. Malik then grabbed the four duffels and they exited the condo heading towards their cars with personal duffle bags slugged over their shoulders. Snatch misjudged his steps, staggering, finally making it to his Porsche truck.

"Bruh, you sure you good? You moving like a zombie right now," Malik asked, knowing the Patron, Ace of Spades, and exotic weed had taken effect on him.

"Yeah, I'm super good. I'm not the one to be questioning about how much alcohol and gas I took in. Jade be the one falling asleep behind the light. Look at her. She barely can make it to her own car. Jade, come ride with me. I'm tryna make history tonight. Let's make a porn video. I know you got that WAP; and you on dat Patron heavy tonight."

"Bruh, you can't be serious right now."

"I'm just putting my true feelings on the table," Snatch interjected. "If you don't step up...then I'm forced to. Somebody gotta be fucking the in-house pussy. She wants you but you running from it." Snatch felt the need to address.

"Bruh, really. You drunk. Slow down for your mouth say something you may regret later," Malik stated, trying his best to consider his words.

"Drunk. I wasn't drunk when you told me you had Jade butt-ass naked at the Marriott, playing in her pussy. No, you too drunk to remember dat," Snatch said loud enough for Jade to hear.

Malik glanced over the hood of the car and made eye contact with Jade before running toward Snatch like a Dodge Ram truck. He grabbed Snatch by the collar, slamming him against the car.

"Malik, Malik!" She called out frightened he would hurt Snatch. "Let him go. He's drunk. You stay saying some crazy shit. I said let him go...Malik!" She screamed.

He continued yelling at Snatch, shaking him violently as Jade yelled over his shoulders. Finally, he stopped and glanced at her.

"Malik, you so outta of character right now. You was just telling us to remain focused, stay in tune, and show love to each other. Now look at you," she said giving him back his own speech in her own words.

"The only reason I ain't gon' slide yo ass is because you drunk, but the next time you disrespect me, it'll be your last...True story." Malik promised.

Snatch nodded in agreement and closed the doors behind him, starting his car, peeling out like a NASCAR driver.

Jade and Malik walked in silence to her car, neither spoke a word until they were in traffic.

"You okay, Malik?" she asked, breaking the silence. "You were definitely wrong for that. I thought you were going to kill him. I don't know who you are at times. You gotta learn how to control your emotions."

"I'm good, the nigga just provoked me. He seemed to have so much to say, so I felt the need to do what he pushed me to do. He better be glad I didn't carry out my alter ego's plan." He confessed.

"So, what stopped you?" Jade asked, knowing the answer.

"The bigger picture for one, and the fact he's family."

"So, the statement he made 'bout you eating my pussy wasn't true?"

"It depends, nosey."

"On what? It's either yes or no."

"Nah, I never told him no shit like that. I told him if it ever came down to it you'd be the front I'd give head to."

Jade sat speechless, moved by his honesty and had a loss for words. "So, you never went down on Asia?"

"Never. Why you find that so hard to believe?"

"Nah, I just didn't know you found me that attractive."

"Jade, through the windows of my eyes you're one of the most attractive women I've ever laid eyes on...and a gangster all in one...but..." He paused.

"But what, Malik? Let's put all of our cards on the table...no secrets. This is a moment of truth...I know you ain't shy?"

"Shy? That may be true, but it's more than that. For me, I'm cautious because I don't want to ruin what we have 'cause it's genuine right now. Anything outside the friend zone will destroy us. It won't end well, 'cause my love for you is deep, so I won't risk our union over a temporary thrill. I need you in my life forever, Jade. It's something in you that I just can't do without. I hope that make sense."

His words penetrated deeply within her, caressing the most sensitive parts of her inner soul, embracing her with everything. She needed to feel his every intention. Jade knew that to cherish a woman's friendship forever took the strength of one's inner soul and that made her feel special than any man had ever made her feel. "Malik," she finally said, trying to hide her rush of emotions. "You too young to know anything about love."

"Love is just an attitude that reveals itself in action. I'm a fool for you and with you. I'll kill for you and run these bands up with you. I am love on all levels."

"But do you really love me? Or are you just whispering those sweet melodies in my ear to get ahead?"

"I was already ahead when you drafted me. I came in with this vision, you just caught my eye in the process," he stated after clearing his throat. "You haven't given me any reason to not love you, and that's the way I want it to be 'til the end, because love is what got us to this level of attraction."

She sat silently as her ears lingered on every word he spoke as if she was a teenage girl on her date. Her emotions swelled to heights they'd never been before. Nothing but this conversation mattered at that moment, with his strong sense of honesty.

"So, in a way, big facts...I do love you, but I'm not in love with you. I love all the wonderful things about you that give me a sense of pleasure being acquainted with you in every way. Your wisdom shines, Jade. You're beautiful yet not the least bit conceited. All these are enduring qualities which attract me very much." He smiled, gaming his way into her heart beyond detection.

Jade gazed into his eyes for a warning sign wanting to look away but couldn't under the circumstances.

"We have too much time invested in us. It took a lot of quality time to get to this level of friendship. I will always cherish what we have experienced together. We mean the world to me. If this ain't love, then love doesn't exist, 'cause we been loving each other all the way through."

Jade was caught up in the moment that she hadn't noticed the light had changed until some chick in a Honda Accord blew her horn. She cursed to herself before pulling off with mixed emotions. "Malik, it's an honor to be in the company of people like yourself, 'cause you're a loyal ass dude, big facts."

"Do you love me?" He asked her.

"Yes, I really do, to the point I even thought about giving you some of this pussy. I'm surprised you never pulled up on me."

"Yeah, right. If that's the case why didn't you just pull up on me?"

"With me it's all about timing. And besides, you wouldn't know how to act." She spoke with confidence.

"Whatever. That pussy ain't like that."

"You right, it ain't all that. It's malicious and delicious. It's that strawberry juice," she said gazing into his eyes.

"Why you keep looking at me like that?"

"I look the way I feel. Ain't nothing wrong with having sex with my best friend."

"Why you talking like that, knowing you ain't gon' follow through."

"Just something I do, I guess."

"Well, you need to find somebody else to tease."

"It's a game we all play."

"Yeah, whatever."

"So, what's the play for tomorrow?"

"I'm a street nigga on a mission right now. I'm tryna run these bands up," he said, reaching into one of the duffle bags, retrieving a handful of money. "Don't we look good together?"

"Boy, bye. How is Asia?" She asked suddenly.

"She super good, outside of getting on my nerves, fussing 'cause I'm always with you. You know how y'all do."

"I don't blame her. I wouldn't trust you around a bitch like me either. So, I feel her pain."

"She be alright," he said as Jade pulled up in front of his condo downtown.

"Look at your drunk ass, can't even get out of the car. You gonna be alright?"

"Yeah, I'm good. Call me tomorrow," he said closing the car door.

She looked at him through the darkness, realizing something much different in the way he said *I love you*. It wasn't the same as before or like any other person. He sounded more direct and sincere with a strong conviction.

After removing the second duffle bag from her trunk, he glanced through the passenger side window and waved goodbye. She placed her fingertips to her lips and blew him a kiss as if it was magical dust. Malik had turned, never seeing the gesture hinting her hidden feelings towards him that she had kept secret for so long.

Malik entered his condo, made it to his master bedroom, dropping the duffle bags. He closed the door and struggled out his clothes, pondering thoughts of his girl Asia. Seconds later he was sound asleep after what seemed like minutes all too soon. Unexpectedly his cell phone started singing, awakening him from his sleep. Rolling over, eyes still closed, he placed the phone to his ear. "Yoooo."

"Top of the morning, daddy," a soft voice on the other end whispered. "You up?"

Recognizing Jade's voice on the other end he tried speaking, but found his throat extra dry. "Yeah, I'm up. What's good?"

"Nothing, just sitting here dying my hair." She was moved by his rich, deep voice sounding manly. "You ready to get this money?"

He slowly sat up in bed, coming to his senses, swinging his feet to the floor, glancing at his Apple Watch. "Damn, it's one o'clock already? Feel like I just went to sleep," he said more to himself than her.

"You ready to get this money, I said?"

"You know I stay ready to get to dis money. But first I need you to take me to Raleigh so I can pick up my car."

"What car you talkin' 'bout? You done bought a car?"

"Yeah, I flew out to Texas to fuck with my peoples over at Mark Motors."

"Stop capping, nigga."

"Nah, I'm for real. Me and Asia's father flew out like three weeks ago."

"Why didn't you take me with you?"

"Girl bye, how would that look?"

"So, what kind of car did you get?"

"That I won't say. You just have to wait and see," he said, flashing a smile she couldn't see.

"Well, I'll be through in an hour."

"Angel Dust," he said.

Instead of saying *one* they always ended their conversations by saying, *Angel Dust* but not this time Jade thought. "Malik?" She said in the most seductive tone she could muster. "I love you more." And pushed the end button, ending the call.

"I got that bitch," he said, taking the phone from his ear and staring at it for a few moments as if he was holding a foreign object.

Jade's voice played back in his mind. "Malik, I love you more." Thinking back on their conversation last night in the car, he began pushing speed dial calling her back but quickly ended the call. He felt like Usher. He had it bad.

He showered and dressed, brushed his teeth and rolled a few blunts, taking one to the head. He was feeling higher than Jay-Z's first album. He stashed the money, made something to eat and called Asia. Moments later, he looked out the window and observed Jade in a sexy all-white 911.

Stepping out of the elevator into the cool sunny air, Malik made his way towards her Porsche as she sat behind the wheel checking out his swagger. Dressed down in a fitted Durham Bull baseball cap, a satin leather Bull Durham jacket over a Bull Durham Jersey and some stitch jeans, highlighting his $3,500 Air Force Ones.

"Damn baby, your dress code is crazy. You don't see niggas rocking no Durham Bulls like that. I love it," he said sincerely meaning it as he descended into the soft leather seat.

"I will wear anything once." He started, popping his collar. "Niggas ain't fucking with me when it comes to being fly."

"Where to?" She asked.

"Swing through the End real quick. I gotta see my nigga. Roc Boy just came home."

"You talking 'bout the one that used to be with Littles?"

"Yeah, that's what them Harlem niggas call him."

"Anyway." She started blowing him off. "Do you remember what you said last night before I dropped you off?"

Unable to recall, he asked.

"Why did I say something that offended you?" He asked, fishing for a clue.

"Nah, I just wanted to see if you remembered. You know how niggas be saying shit they really don't mean. Especially, when they're under the influence."

"Facts," he agreed.

Jade sat dressed provocatively in a lambskin motorcycle jacket by D&G, and some jeans that fitted her thighs perfectly. So much so they aroused a sensual sexual desire of interest to the point where he could tell she wore no panties underneath them.

"You like my jacket, Malik?" She asked knowing he had noticed.

"I'm loving the pants as well, but you know I'ma foot man. Yo' shoe game is crazy."

She pulled up in front of a newer modeled house on Rosedale. The whole hood seemed to be out since it was The West End Reunion.

"Damn, everybody from the old to the new school out dis bitch." Malik started, stepping out the car.

"Yo Malik, Keese said what up," Teddy stated in regards to a hood general on lock down doing a life sentence.

"Tell bruh I said what up. He good?" Malik asked, concerned.

"He tryna pay his lawyer off so he can come home," Teddy said. "This his daughter right here."

Malik reached into his Louis Vuitton backpack and pulled out fifty neat one hundred bills, and walked over towards Keese's daughter and handed to her. "Here, this for you," he said handing her an additional five hundred dollars. "If your daddy needs anything, call me. I fucks with your daddy. Big Facts."

He ran in the house only to return seconds later noticing Carla, Jade's BBF sitting in the front seat, so he jumped in alongside her. "Take me to get my car."

Thirty minutes later, Jade was pulling into the Detail Shop in Raleigh.

"Damn bitch, who Flying Spur is that?" Carla asked Jade.

"Don't get me to lie, but whoever driving that getting to the bag," Jade said as Malik jumped out heading inside Tint World.

He returned followed by the store owner, with a Bentley key in his hand. He pressed down on a button attached to the key. Unlocking the doors to the Flying Spur, the owner showed Malik how to work the hidden compartment, which could be used as a stash box.

"Yo, Jade, pull up real quick." He motioned for her to come over.

"Malik, this you?" Jade asked, impressed.

"Yeah, you like it."

"Can I drive it for a day?" She asked wanting to be the first bitch seen breezing through in Malik's spaceship.

"Just let me be the bitch in the passenger. I'm good," Carla said, mesmerized by his favor.

"Hold up. I'll be right back," Malik told both exotic roses as he went inside to pay the owner who personally did all the detailing, add the twenty-two inch chrome rims, alarm, sound system and candy paint job. He had invested an additional sixty thousand in it. "Jade, we got a least an hour before we have to meet up with Ceelo," he said as he returned to his car.

Jade was bent over looking in the car with both hands on the driver side seat exposing her perfectly heart shaped ass in the air. Malik had never seen her in that position. He was amazed at how the designer label highlighted her new body, restraining her shape. Exotic dreams flashed through his mind like still pictures, as the banana between his legs revealed itself through his jeans. Jade was marvelous and sensual. Now, he had to have her sexually.

"Facts, so let me get missing. I have a lot to do," she said, removing her head from the inside of the car, spinning to face him. "You have great taste, Malik. I'm impressed."

"It's nothing," he responded.

She looked at him with a puzzled look masking her face.

"Call me later, Jade."

"Okay baby, Angel Dust," she said noticing a semi hard erection in his pants. She was now aware he had been watching her new shape, and it was only a matter of time before that he would be all hers.

"Say it two times," he said as he pulled into Capital Blvd. traffic.

Chapter 9

Jade's 911 was extremely clean as she cruised the inner streets of Durham. She spotted Castro's Porsche with the Ashanti wheels a couple cars ahead of her. She hit her turn signal changing lanes and came to a stop alongside him, blowing the horn trying to get his attention. Looking over his shoulder, he lowered his window. Music blasted ghetto flavor from the sound system as he and Snatch nodded to 21 Savage feat Future.

"Red Rum Salute!" Snatch yelled through the window, looking like a million dollars.

"Red Rum Salute. Y'all niggas think y'all superstars don't cha?" She yelled starting over thunderous beats. "Turn that shit down."

Before he could respond, the light changed green.

"Follow me," she said, motioning with her hand.

Castro pulled off behind her, following her into Phoenix Square parking lot.

"Where you coming from?" Castro yelled, pulling alongside her.

"U-Neak Boutique," she responded by lying. She concealed the fact she had just collected 75,000 from one of Ceelo's workers.

"Where you two demons headed?" She asked being nosey.

"I'm 'bout to drop Snatch of at his car and go fuck something."

"Boy bye, you ain't fucking nothing worth fucking." She started joking, because lately she had seen him with a different chick.

"You got me fucked up. I get mo' ass than the average surgeon."

"Yo Sis, I need to holla at cha'," Snatch said as he opened the suicide style door, hopping out of one Porsche into another one.

"Bruh, you good because I'm 'bout to slide." Castro asked.

"Yeah, I'm good, bruh," Snatch said while closing the Jade's passenger side door, sliding onto the leather seats.

"Holla at me later," Castro said before pulling off.

Jade looked at her watch, noticing it was 3:30 pm. She cursed herself knowing she had to meet Ceelo at South Point Mall to deliver the money. Wondering what Snatch needed to talk to her about, she looked over at him. " What's on your mind?" She asked, looking through her peripheral. "You up to something."

"I stay on demon time. And why you out here on the track with all this money on you?" He asked, looking into the duffle.

"I had to make a run for Ceelo."

"Oh, word."

"Yeah," she simply said.

"That's what's up... But yo, I need a favor. You think you can make something happen for me?" He said, hoping she would say, "Yeah, take what's in the bag."

"I'm working, but you gotta be patient."

"I understand that, but my pockets getting low," he barked at her. "I got at most twenty-five hundred left, and you know my spending habit is unbalanced right now," he said, sounding angry as he pulled out the money counting it in front of her, as if she was the reason for him spending so much.

"First of all, you need to tone your voice down. I don't know who you think you talking to like that. I told you I gotcha, but truthfully, I don't owe you shit," she said feeling bad for him cause being broke doesn't feel good. "What the fuck you doing with your money? Why can't you get it together like Castro and Malik. I told you not to cop that Porsche truck but you had to have it. You splurge too much. Now you sitting here looking dumbfounded. I know you like to look fly, and splurge on the bitches but get to the bag first. Them bitches ain't going nowhere. That's one thing you ain't never gotta worry about. A bitch gone always be around," she said hoping he was listening.

"Big Facts, but I need a brick or two," he spoke changing the subject. "But let me do me. If I feel like stunting, let me stunt. It's my life."

"Yeah, you right it is your life, but I ain't gone keep going in my stash to make you feel good or keep risking my life so you can splurge on some bitch." She added, pulling up to the corner of South and Enterprise St. "Hit me later. I'll have something for you."

"Yeah right, Ms. Philosopher," he barked exiting the vehicle slamming the door shut.

***

Jade sat silently in South Point Mall's parking lot patiently awaiting Ceelo's arrival. Suddenly, Ceelo and Malik pulled up in a black over black Benz wagon. Ceelo blew his horn motioning for Jade to follow him. She followed behind the AMG wagon pulling over and stepped out looking so fly as her D&G shades were casually perched atop her head as she approached the vehicle with the duffle bag climbing in the backseat.

"What up, baby girl? Everything work out for you?"

"Facts...everybody came through but the nigga Trouble. He said he'll see you tonight." She smiled. "Hey Malik." She said, raising her hand greeting him.

"Red Rum Salute."

His response sounded slightly irrigated by the fact that he felt that Jade and Ceelo were more than just business partners.

"How much work you got left?" Ceelo questioned.

"Like a half of cake. That shit already sold though. I just gotta meet her."

"Who ole girl from the Mac?"

"Yeah."

"Aight cool," he said, reaching for the duffle and glancing inside it. "Jade, I appreciate all you do for the team. I can honestly say you get to the money with no losses, shorts, or excuses. I love you for that," he said warmly with praise.

Malik looked around locking eyes with Jade as she instantly read his mind. She sent him a quick message, licking her lips and hoping to remove his insecurities. However, his countenance remained emotionless towards her actions.

"Well, being it's Friday, what we doing tonight?" She said changing the subject.

"Jim Jones is supposed to come through tonight, so I'm heading out to Raleigh," Ceelo responded.

"Yeah I heard Dip Set supposed to come through. I might pull up," Malik said.

"Come on Malik you don't ever go out," she spoke.

"Shit, fuck the club. I ain't made it yet."

"I can't tell, Malik. You got that Bentley."

"You know I had to fuck up this cash on a new toy."

"So, what's next Money Grip?"

"More money, more problems, and fulfilling my promises." Malik started prophesying his future.

They exchanged a few more words then Jade slid out back into her Porsche heading back to her castle.

***

Back at the stash house, Ceelo examined the contents of the bag to determine the amount of money it contained, when his cell rang. "Yo, what up?" He responded.

"Yo, this Hysheem, what's up?" Spoke to one of his workers from the South.

"Oh, what up my dude?"

"You coming through?"

Nah, my people will be through though," Ceelo responded, refusing to discuss the matter any further on the phone. He never talked recklessly over the wire.

"Say no more."

"One." Ceelo ended the call. He called Malik.

"Talk to me," Malik said upon answering the call.

"Yo, I need you to slide through Hollywood."

"I'm on it," Malik responded.

"Aight," Ceelo shot back, ending the call.

Pulling up at the corner of South and Enterprise in his Bentley for the first time blasting "Feeling It," a classic from Jay-Z's first album Reasonable Doubt, his system turned everyone's head. Malik was really feeling himself. Before pulling off he stared at the hustlers, divas, red shooters, and fiends until he spotted who he came to see.

"Yo, Snatch." He yelled out the window.

Snatch turned around noticing the candy paint Bentley sitting on chrome and his mouth dropped.

"Bruh… you a fool for that," he said, shocked running towards the car.

"Where Hysheem?" Malik asked as niggas and bitches crowded around to get a better view at his slick Bentley.

"Hold up. I'll take you to him." He turned around and motioned for his B.M. to bring him his four-fifth which she kept tucked in her Fendi bag.

His baby mother approached and passed him his ratchet. He jumped into the car looking around. *Malik was fulfilling his dreams,* he thought to himself.

"Dis you?" He asked, wanting one himself.

"Yeeaah," he said as he eyed A.D. in designer jeans and a pair of Retro Jordan's. "Where Hysheem?"

"Round on Hollywood," he said reclining back.

Malik made a U-turn as if he owned the street and flew past the on looking crowd towards Umstead St.

"Pull over tight here," Snatch said, pointing to the curb in front of Hysheem grandmother's house. "Yo, Hy." He yelled as Malik stopped in the middle of the street. Hysheem opened the screen door and ran down the stairs towards the car.

"What it do, five?"

"You already know," Malik spoke as he handed Hysheem five ounces of heroin. In return, Hysheem handed him a bag of money. "Call me later," Malik said.

"Say less," he responded. "Dis you?" He said, eyeing the Bentley.

"Yeah. Let me get off this block. We gone holla." He pulled off. "So, what been up with you?"

"Slinging crime," Snatch said, fumbling through his phone. "What about you? What you been up to?"

"Just tryna get in position most dudes ain't in, you dig bruh?"

"Facts... but why is it so hard for a nigga like me to get in position?"

"Only you can answer that. Shit takes time, five. You can't just sprint through this shit. It's a marathon. Sometimes you gotta run through this shit, then fall back and catch your breath. But as long as you on the track, you can win," Malik said, enlightening his comrade. "When Jade first introduced me to this food, I fed all my niggas and spread the cheddar around. You should be extra good by now, but you not cause you blowing unnecessary money on bitches and lawyers, fighting them petty ass cases you be catching and a lot of other bullshit."

I ain't gone front. If the pussy good, I'm spending money on it."

Facts. I do it all the time. If my bitch want dis Louis bag, she can get it. Anything she wants, she can get it, but I'm in position to do that because I got an appetite to be richer than I was yesterday. I thirst for power, therefore, I'll never let anything or anyone get in the way of me accomplishing my dream. That's gotta be your aim, bruh."

Snatch nodded in agreement as Malik enlightened him on street-preneurship, knowing that in order to organize and operate a hundred grand a day operation, it demanded hard work, discipline and desire.

"Stay away from dem fuck niggas, and just get to the bag. That should be your focus... your only focus. Become a money magnet and surround yourself with niggas that has the same goals you got. That's how you forge ahead and prestige," Malik said, trying to give his comrade the blueprint.

"Big Facts..." Snatch agreed. "I do need to disassociate myself from niggas that don't mean me no good, especially that nigga Jazzie. Bruh, did I tell you how dis nigga fucked up a half of cake?"

"You can't be serious right now. Where he at now?" Malik stated harshly.

"Snicker told me he be on D-block."

"What? On Dawkins? Where Kenny Wayne and Penny stay?"

"Bruh, how you know where Penny stay at? Let me find out you be sliding in that late night."

"Bruh, I'ma keep it a band. She smack but she got that wet wet."

Snatch burst out laughing. "Big Facts...but that's where he be at."

"Does Castro know about this?" Malik stated, pulling out his phone to call Castro to inform him of the information he just received concerning Jazzie. Having come up with a plan, Malik discussed the matter with both counterparts, advising them on how the situation should be handled. Shortly after, he hung up, switched vehicles, met up with Castro and headed over towards Dawkins.

Malik pulled the Honda onto Dawkins and parked behind Jazzie's Lexus. He eyed the New York breed as Snatch exited the vehicle to approach him.

"What up, son?" Jazzie asked as Snatch walked on the porch.

"You son," Snatch said, imitating him. "You remember I was telling you about my man with the low prices. Well he's straight now. What you tryna do?"

"That's son right dere? Jazzie asked, pointing towards the Honda Accord Wagon.

"Yeah, that's him."

"Oh aight...yo G.I., hold me down son," Jazzie said, indicating for G.I. to hold the trap down.

"Bruh, dis Jazzie, the one I was telling you about. He got D-block in the head lock," Snatch said as they approached the car.

"What up son?" Jazzie said coming on like a tough guy.

"What it do?" Malik stated extended his hand out the window. "My man tells me you got shit on smash round here. I'm tryna put some food on your table."

"How much you talking?"

"Yo, I don't do business like this. Get in, let's ride," Malik said as Castro opened the back door for Jazzie to get in.

Discovering that the job would be easy, Castro decided to play along and maintain his cool.

"So, what can you handle?" Malik asked, baiting the hook.

"Whatever. What you got?" Jazzie said, closing the car door. Malik pulled off.

"You think you can handle a half of cake?" Malik asked, just throwing a number out there.

"Fuck no. That nigga can't handle no half of cake. He couldn't even handle the shit bruh gave him," Castro said putting his 44 magnum in the Jazzie's side warning him not to struggle. "What type of time you on?"

Castro relieved him of his gun, informing him if he tried anything he would murk him on sight.

They spent the next thirty minutes driving in silence. Malik suddenly spoke as he pulled in behind a secluded house they often used to fight dogs in.

"Get the fuck out my car," Malik barked. "You know it's over for you right?"

Jazzie tried to explain himself, but was cut short when Snatch bitch slapped him to the ground with his Ruger. "Ain't no need to plead now nigga, getcha bitch ass up," Snatch said standing over him.

"Snatch, take his bitch ass in the house before he wakes the neighbors with all that screaming," Malik said.

Jazzie, having met Malik only moments ago, feared for his life. He had heard many he said she said stories concerning Malik's past about how niggas that crossed him turned up missing. With these thoughts, he stood to his feet and tried pleading for his life.

"Look man, look. I got the money at my crib." He pleaded as he eyed the silver and black Ruger Malik held in his hand. "Snatch, dis me homie. Don't let this shit go down, bruh. I can make one call and get you your money," he said as tears formed in his eyes.

"Nigga, dis ain't 'bout no motherfucking money. It's about respect. When you disrespect my man, you disrespect me, and when you disrespect me, the penalty is death."

"Do what you do best, son. You gone kill me anyway," Jazzie said letting Malik know that he wasn't scared to die. "That pistol in your palm doesn't make you real."

As they entered the house, Malik went straight to the kitchen and opened all the cabinets.

Removing the small bag, he found a syringe and a gram of heroin laced with fentanyl and placed the contents on the table. Jazzie began sweating and looking for a way to escape but his chances were slim to none.

"You try anything stupid and I'ma slump you myself," Malik warned. "No cap, I need you to try dis new shit out for me."

Jazzie sat motionless trying to think of a way out of this abnormal situation, as thoughts ran rapidly through his mind. However, the cold steel to his head frightened him.

"Today's your lucky day, gangster. I'm about to dump so much of this shit into your system, you gone feel like a zombie." Malik laughed, inserting the needle into Jazzie's arms.

Suddenly, Jazzie started shaking violently. His eyes rolled in the back of his head upwards as if he was praying to God just before he crashed to the floor. His violent shaking continued then abruptly ceased.

"Should I finish him off?" Snatch said, pointing the gun to his head.

"Nah, he's already dead. Let's get outta here," Malik said before walking circumspectly out the side door.

Chapter 10

The Sport Bar was a prestigious nightclub located in Raleigh, North Carolina. On this particular night, it was in an uproar. Full to capacity, shoulder to shoulder. Big Party! BIGGER names! Lotsa liquor!

The entire club shouted continuously as the DJ changed the songs smoothly, increasing the energetic crowd as they danced to the latest music in their designer labels as if it was a fashion show event.

The bar was lined with vast bottles of Ace of Spades, Rum, Patron, and more as the two college students served drinks behind the counter to customers providing a mood change in their night of fun and dancing, balling like the words of Jim Jones.

Off to the right of the bar, a small group of New Yorkers stood like hood millionaires as they each held Styrofoam cups in one hand and a bottle of Ace of Spades in the other, as they chatted with excitement.

"Yo, I thought yo man was coming through?" The young felon with dreads asked Ceelo.

"He probably won't even show. He don't be doing the club like that," Ceelo said.

Outside the club, Malik breezed through the crowded parking lot looking for a place to park his giant Bentley. After circling the lot several times, he finally found an empty parking space between a Luxury Edition Aston Martin and a Mercedes Benz. He killed the engine and secured the car, arming the alarm system.

"Hey handsome." A young diva wearing an extremely tight *Come Fuck Me* skirt said while sashaying her way past him.

Turning to acknowledge who was speaking, he noticed the five-foot-four Shaw University college student with a tropical look eyeing him over her shoulder while walking with a gang of potentials. He hadn't seen the diva before a day in his life, so he decided to investigate further.

"Excuse me miss with the gorgeous face," he said approaching as she stood in the long waiting line. "What's your name?"

"Nikki." She started smiling.

"How you living, Nikki?"

"Independently." She started batting her eyes. "Why you ask?"

"Just curious. So, what do you do to maintain your independence?

"Right now I'm modeling part time, due to my commitment to school."

"What school you go to?" Malik asked to cut her off.

"Shaw University," she said as she turned back around to face her friends.

"Damn, you thick as fuck," he mumbled looking down at her skirt that captured her shape.

"I heard that," she said blushing.

"No Cap. Your thighs are but one part of a wonderful work of living art."

"Facts... I hear that a lot. Guys seem to celebrate my curves everywhere I go."

"I definitely can understand why," he said, making her smile. "Just being able to converse with you is a thrilling experience."

"I see you a charmer."

"I'm just a man that love to tell a woman beautiful thangs, but I also have other appealing qualities as well," he said making eye contact. "I don't defuse that, but this is a different level of success. But already know, you know money when you see money," he stated with hopes she could see the life he was living. "Do you have obligations to someone?"

"Yes, I do have someone special in my life, but it's not serious like that," she said hoping he could see what she was looking for in a man.

"What would it take for a man like me to court a woman like you?"

"Quality time and money," she said sincerely.

"That's dope. You just spit some real shit. I can fuck with you," he stated, meaning every word. "I have a question. What's your view on independence?"

"To me, it means pursuing a glamorous, extravagant lifestyle. What about you? What's your take on independence?"

"To me it means freedom to explore new horizons." He paused to allow his words to sink deep into her mind. "It's obvious we have different views on independence, which allows me to understand how our conversation started off on such a high note. You're basically interested strictly on yourself, whereas I'm more interested in the world."

"Big Facts..." She said with excitement. "I deserve the best of everything. I'm more physical, especially when getting to the bag." She spoke with motivation.

"We will see. Can we exchange numbers?"

"Only if you promise to call."

"That should be your least worry," he said reaching into his pockets retrieving large sums of crisps blue faces. "Drinks on me," he said handing Nikki and her crew of seven, three hundred dollars apiece to fully enjoy themselves.

"I bet you do. I done heard it all before." She started sounding like Sunshine Anderson.

Glancing around the club he noticed it was full to capacity, with seven women to every man. Corny niggas eyed him with jealousy and envy as he made his way through the crowd living the dream with no security following him.

Dressed down a colorful jacket, scarf, jeans belt and sneakers all made by Gucci, with a diamond choker chain with a diamond encrusted Bentley key, he maneuvered his way through with his charismatic presence towards a gang of gentleman with qualities controlling the bar area who appeared to his acquaintance, Ceelo and his army.

"What's dope boy?" Ceelo said, saluting his new general. "Have a drink," he said, handing him a bottle of Ace of Spades.

"Ain't nothing in here but exotic skittles tonight," Malik said, popping his bottle, observing the most attractive women he had ever seen. "Everything in here is high class dimension."

"It's crazy right." Ceelo added. "The Sports Bar stays packed with potential, especially when celebrities pull up."

"I'm impressed."

"Son, dis my man Lucky."

Malik eyed the young shooter noticing he was definitely built for this street life. Dressed down in Gucci Red with diamonds in his ear the size of golf balls.

"What's popping, five?" Malik stated out of respect.

We popping blood?" Lucky shot back with a thick New York accent.

"Yo Malik, you know yo' man Meek Mill gone pull up tonight.

"Nigga quick playing," Malik said with excitement.

"No cap. Lucky fucks with Meek hard so we made her that happen for you." Ceelo started showing his love and appreciation for Malik's drive to make things happen.

"Yo Ceelo, who is shorty in the yellow catsuit?" Malik asked.

"Oh, that's Notorious. She's hot, isn't she?"

"Damn right and more. She leaving with me tonight," Malik responded lustfully.

"That's all good too, but shorty puts on for the city in the club," Ceelo assured him.

Malik maintained silence as he watched her like a hawk, admiring her natural beauty and elegance. He couldn't believe how much she resembled Lauren London. The only difference she was petite and much curvier.

Malik motioned for the bartender to come over and ordered bottles of Patron for Notorious and her crew of diamonds. He finessed his way over and made contact with the woman, who was summertime fine. Upon noticing him, the laughter abruptly ceased.

"Hello, beautiful. Even though it's winter, you summertime fine." He started, holding his bottle slightly before his lips.

"You not so bad yourself. I like your chain," she said softly, rubbing her hand against the Bentley key.

Malik sipped as she eyed him with a gleam in her eyes and demeanor. "Whatever. I'm trying to get to know the diva behind the pretty stare." He started knowing she was wearing a mask.

Astonished by his gesture, she downed the shot glass of booze and excused herself, to be alone with the zookeeper.

"So, you trying to explore me?"

"You can say that. So, what's your name?"

"Notorious...and yours?"

"Malik."

"So, what you trying to get into tonight, Notorious?" He asked, slipping his hand below his waist hooking his belt buckle.

"That all depends," She said smiling.

"On what?"

"On what you trying to do, and what's in it for me. That yellow Aston Martin parked outside didn't come free."

"Oh, that's you?" He asked.

"Yeah, for now, until I can upgrade my shit to a Bentley coupe."

"I'm parked right beside you. What a coincidence."

"Let's cut the small talk...whatcha tryna do?" She asked placing her hand on her hips shifting her weight on one leg.

"I'm tryna toss a few dollars," he said reaching into his pocket pulling out a stack of hundreds tossing it in the air. "This shit chump change. I make it rain for fun."

Her eyes widened as she looked up, refusing to divert from locking eyes with them. Not knowing how to respond, she looked down at her friends as they were scraping up the money from off the floor as they indicated that she needed to go handle her business because he was a real boss. She then grabbed Malik by the hand and made her way through the crowd headed to the nearest restroom. "Excuse me, excuse me," she shouted continuously as she shunned her way through the crowd.

Once she reached her destination, she searched for an empty stall and pushed Malik inside.

"Bitch, what you looking at? Don't act like you never handled your business in the club!" She shouted to the woman standing at the sink being extra nosey.

Malik laughed. "I like you already," he said looking into her eyes as she sat on the toilet.

She quickly unzipped Malik's pants and went to his banana as if it was a place of worship. "I might can't handle all this," she whispered, working his enormous member to its full size.

Staring at its length in amazement, she began to feel dampness between her inner thighs wetting the crotch of her panties. She pulled him closer, wrapping her lips around the head of his monster dick smearing her candy yellow lip gloss on his swollen gland, as he slowly began stabbing his erect penis in and out of her mouth, feeling the warm wetness as if he was inside her imagination.

She grabbed his ass, pulling him deeper into her mouth until she felt his nuts slapping against her chin and filling her throat with all of him. She arched her neck upwards deep throating him, as he climaxed all of his frustration into her mouth. His legs became like rubber bands as he struggled to remain standing. Suddenly, he crashed on the door completely drained by Notorious frantic suction methods.

"Do you like it?" She asked, wiping her mouth with the back side of her hand as she began to leave.

"Of course, but I'm still tryna see you tonight though," he said, handing her five hundred dollars, before making their way back through the screaming crowd towards the bar.

"Red Rum Salute," Castro greeted his confidant. "Who you got witcha? He quizzed, eyeballing Notorious.

"Oh, she's the newest member to the team of animals," Malik stated with confidence.

Jade stood in silence eyeing Malik. Seeing Notorious with him didn't sit well with her for some odd reason. She had an idea Notorious had worked her wonders, however, she decided not to interfere in his social life, because he had to learn life through life experiences.

"Red Rum Salute," Malik saluted Jade noticing her demeanor had changed. "You alright?"

"I'll be fine. Ain't shit I can't handle." She reminded him.

"You got a minute?"

Before she could respond, a female ran over hollering loudly, grabbing a bottle of Champagne by the neck and swung it violently at the back of Snatch's head, who was unaware he was being ambushed by one of his bitches.

"Snatch!" Jade yelled pushing him out of the way just as the woman cocked the bottle back.

As the woman missed, she damn near caught Jade in the face. The crowd suddenly panicked, stampeding towards the action.

"Beat that bitch ass," a voice yelled out. Jade wrestled the woman to the floor grunting like an animal as they tried to subdue each other.

"Bitch! Let my hair go!" One of them yelled as Jade rolled on top of her, grabbing the opportunity she threw a short left punch towards the woman's face. However, the woman deflected it with her wrist and instantly covered her head, knowing she had to get Jade off before she was badly beaten.

The woman raised her back attempting to sit up and punched Jade in the chin. Jade's head snapped back sharply as the woman pushed her off. They both jumped to their feet. Jade raised her clenching fist and with blinding speed, she punched her in the mouth, drawing blood instantly, then followed with her left, missing as the woman ducked grabbing her around the waist. Struggling, both women crashed on the floor a second time. Jade this time landed underneath her. The woman punched Jade in the nose, drawing blood. Jade grunted as pain shot through her entire face. She grabbed the woman by both wrists and wrestled her down. When someone poured a bottle of Patron on both of them, Malik caught the individual in the act and crashed a powerful right punch into the man's mouth, knocking out his front teeth. Before he could recover, Snatch, Lucky, and Castro started stomping the football player as Malik stopped both women from fighting.

"He got a gun!" A woman's voice yelled.

In a crazed panic, people started rushing for the door toppling over one another. Malik pulled Jade to the floor, protecting her from any danger. Pulling his gun out as shots echoed throughout the club. Jade screamed desperately trying to hide under her shielding body. She was hysterical and began regretting she hadn't snuck her own gun in just as Malik had done. Another shot was fired as plaster speckled down from the ceiling to the floor.

"Where the fuck is Castro at?" Snatch asked as he caught up with Jade and Malik. "I done looked everywhere for bruh."

"He probably outside by now," Malik said as he kept his gun out of sight but to the ready.

He scanned the area of the parking lot noticing people running to their cars. Malik, Jade and Snatch did the same.

Moments later, Malik pulled up behind a Benz as two hooded felons ran up beside the AMG on both sides. He watched as they emptied their pistols through the windows, killing the driver in a well-executed cross fire.

Oh shit!" Malik grasped in shock as the two figures that moved similar to Castro and Lucky jumped into a BMW that donned New York tags reading *Lucky.*

Chapter 11

The very next day, Castro pulled up into the BP Gas Station on Alston Ave to get gas. Stepping out of his new solid colored McLaren 720S Spider, he was wearing a hoodie and cargo pants by Dior with a pair of New Balance laced loosely matched by a similar colored scarf tucked into his back pocket. His caramel skin tone, thick eyebrows highlighted his slightly gentlemanly swag.

Suddenly his phone sounded, catching his undivided attention. Seconds later, he lifted his phone and began conversing with a potential dope boy from McDougal Terrence Projects. After setting up a major play, he observed his surroundings before entering the store. He paid for his gas bill and exited the hood trap store. As he walked circumspectly towards his spaceship, he noticed two poetic masterpieces lounging in a similar McLaren as his very own, eyeing him behind designer shades closely. He internalized both women as he filled his tank with fuel.

Moments later, he eased his way onto his carbon fiber seats, hit push start, and pulled alongside the passenger side of the McLaren.

"Where you two college cheerleaders headed too?" He asked, flashing a smile of flamboyance.

"To the Louis Vuitton store in Charlotte. You wanna follow us?" The passenger said, letting him know it was all about getting to the bag.

"If that's what it takes to court you, I'm in," he responded with a shot like Curry in the finals.

"Look at you, ready to spend some money. I'm just fucking with you..."

"Look at you, ready to spend some money. She was just fucking with you," the driver said, lifting her Dior shades from her eyes. "We 'bout to go get something to eat at Ruth Chris."

"May I join YOU, my treat?" He was mesmerized by the ocean waves in her eyes.

"Sure. Why not? Follow ME," she said softly, pulling off as he followed close behind listening to Drake.

Once at the restaurant they entered and found a place to sit. Castro ordered the ladies drinks and had a Bacardi 151 and cranberry with a twist of lemon for himself. The driver asked where he was from. As he turned to answer her, it dawned on him that they had actually crossed paths in the past. He was speechless for a moment thinking she might have recognized him and remembered what transpired during their time together. He suddenly became skittery in her presence.

"What's wrong? Your demeanor has changed since we sat down," she explained letting him know that she had been observing him the whole while.

"Nah, I'm good," he responded, refusing to make eye contact anymore.

"Let me find out you shy," the passenger said, slashing into what he had to say.

"Me... Never that," he said.

"So, where you from?" She asked a second time.

"L.A," he said lying, hoping she didn't ask him about any locations, because he knew of none.

"Oh really. I've been there a few times," she responded. "So, what do they call you?"

"Oh, Castro, and you?" He asked, staring at them both.

"I'm Joel and this is my girlfriend, Destiny."

"Oh okay," he simply said.

Joel showed a great deal of interest in Castro, as she continuously asked personal questions. The more she asked, the more over suspicious he became with concern she would remember him.

However, he kept his gangsterism intact and smoothly collected his thoughts before revealing what was on his heart.

Constantly alluring her with beautiful words, she remained under his spell until he convinced himself. Unexpectedly, his phone rang during their meal. He excused himself before answering the call, discovering it to be Snatch as he ducked off into the men's restroom.

"Red Rum Salute." Castro started saluting his shadow.

"Red Rum Salute," Snatch said, anxious to get his next question in. Bruh, you got sum more pillows left?"

"Yeah, how many..? Bruh, guess what..." He abruptly started catching himself, as he was about to brief Snatch about the situation with Joel, but decided against it.

"Spit it out nigga."

"Nah, now is not the right time, but I'll let you know what just pulled up out of nowhere. You driving?"

"Nah, I let my B.M. drive my shit. I'm gliding through the city with Malik."

"Y'all niggas pull up." Castro mentioned so Snatch could see what the wind blew in.

"Where you at?"

"Ruth Chris out by South Point."

"Say less. Angel Dust gang."

"Say it two times."

After ending the call, Castro returned to the table to finish entertaining the two unique females. Joel stood to excuse herself from the table when Castro's phone suddenly rang a second time.

"Who the fuck calling me private?" He mumbled to himself. "Who dis?" He asked curious to know who would call him from an unknown number.

"Look, I got the drop on you and dat bitch. I want a hunnit bands or you both die," an abnormal voice, strange and eerily ordered.

Castro scanned Destiny's countenance, noticing an infrared dot the size of a skittle. "Dis shit for real," he mumbled as he pulled the phone from his ear, turned and glanced out the window in the direction he thought the red beam was coming from. A yellow Aston Martin Vanquish sat bow legged in the parking lot with an infrared beaming from the passenger side window. Slowly standing, he motioned to leave when Destiny noticed fear in his eyes.

"Is everything okay?"

He remained uncommunicative as he began marching towards the entrance door.

Malik and Snatch maneuvered their way from the comfort of their seats on joke time.

"You see how dat shit feels now," Snatch stated comically. Castro approached his confidants considering ways to repay them both.

"Y'all niggas on joke time I see."

Joel had returned from the ladies room and stood in silence monitoring Castro and his confidants with a watchful eye. *I like the way he move.* She thought as she admired his charismatic demeanor.

"So, what's your take on Castro?" Joel asked Destiny.

"He's definitely your type." Destiny admitted. "But who is that driving?" She asked, showing interest.

Oh, that's the same guy I was telling you about that I saw with Ceelo the other day," Joel responded fixing her hair.

"He looks like he be getting to the bag."

"Big Facts... and he cute."

"Come on girl, let's go be nosey," Destiny said with a curious gaze in her eyes.

"Castro," Joel said as she sauntered her way through the exit door with a warm smile, holding a hundred dollar bill in her hand approaching him. "Do you have any small bills?" She asked.

"I'll handle the bill, shorty. Let me holla at my people real quick," he said, turning to face her. As a matter fact, here." He started, handing her three hundred dollars. She accepted the money and turned to leave.

"Bruh, what type of time you on? That's the bitch from the home invasion." Snatch started with a weird gaze at Castro.

"Bruh, I got dis. She don't remember me. Facts."

"Bruh, that bitch knows, trust me. I wouldn't advise you to fuck with that bitch, dawg.

" Bruh, I'm good. You still want that pillow?" Castro asked, trying to change the subject.

"Facts. That's the only way I can function."

"This batch from that new connect I was telling you about from out West," Castro said, walking over towards his spaceship to retrieve a pound of weed for his man to blow on. Snatch regrouped and folded onto the soft leather. Malik was on a prison call building with Keese on some next level shit. He always took time out to converse with real homes from the city.

Moments later, Castro returned with a Louis Vuitton backpack and handed to Snatch, who at the time was kicking the shit with this Nurse he had relations with, while at Warren Correctional. " Good looking homie," Snatch said, peeping into the backpack. "Bruh, slide through Henderson tonight. I got something for us set up with some real Gorillas."

"I'm feeling that. I love them country bitches who possess an unrivaled beauty."

"Bruh, you riding round with all them pillows?" Snatch asked concerned for his mentor.

"Bruh, I don't fear shit but them indictment papers. You know how I live. I just got my recreational license to dispense weed legally, so we good," Castro stated, nodding to that Winning Music by Lil Baby. "What y'all real niggas 'bout to get into?"

"I'm 'bout to go spend some quality time with this potential workhorse," Malik said reflecting on his night with Notorious at the Hilton.

"Who? That rainbow from last night?" Castro said, realizing whose car he was driving.

"All the heaven I need to see," Malik said knowing he had just crossed paths with a unique woman with an overwhelming charm.

"They say she moving dem pillows, but that's between me and you," Castro said sowing seeds of violence.

"It is what it is. The streets stay whispering. I hope she is getting to the bag. There's enough in the streets for all of us," Malik said speaking in code.

"I'm tryna get active. Where that bitch stay at?" Snatch asked.

"I ain't gone even respond to that." Malik started wondering what type time Snatch was on.

"I know right. Bruh stay on demon time. Snatch, you sounding real desperate right now. A yo, I'm 'bout to chill with my new friends," Castro said, walking backwards from the car. "Angel Dust."

"Say it two times," Malik and Snatch said in unison.

Castro approached Joel and Destiny who seemed to be in deep conversation enjoying the atmosphere.

"My bad ladies. So, what y'all bout to get into?" Wanna go catch a Hornets game tonight?" Castro asked, mesmerized by Joel's eyes. She had the most direct, deep, interesting eyes. The kind of woman Castro could court for a lifetime.

"I would love to go see Zion Williamson take on the Hornets, but Des have to work and I need to settle down so I can study for my exams tomorrow," she said sharing more of her responsibilities.

"What school do you go to?"

"Eagle Pride, Eagle Pride." They shared simultaneously. "Big Facts. I fucks with Central. You ever heard of Jamal Elliot? The running back for the eagles? That's my man son."

Without uttering a word, Joel handed Destiny the keys as they were leaving and headed over towards Castro's car.

"There's something that I would like to say to you, that I consider to be of vital importance," he said leaning against his McLaren. "First of all, I wish to express how very happy I am to be able to stand in the midst of your lovingness. It is an honor as well a pleasure while I am here talking to you." He started dripping his best sauce. "I am hoping that you will absorb some of this automatic upcoming compassion, real love, and real romance that will be running about every loving word that I speak to you. I also want you to understand that there is no falsehood of any proportion in what I am saying to you because my desire to get to know you is most truthful, abiding, and faithful, unshakeable, and free from nonsense."

Moved by his words, Joel was unable to respond because she had never concerned herself with anyone behind Ceelo's back. However, a part of her knew better, but her heart screamed to do better.

"I don't know..." She paused to gather her emotions. "I'm really busy with school right now, and besides I have a man."

I understand that, but what does he have to do with us? Our time together is our time." He swore.

"I like that," she said smiling. "But honestly, it's hard to say at the moment even though he rarely has time for me," she said warmly locking eyes giving the indication of a possibility.

"Well take this. The next time you get lonely and need to pillow talk, give me a call," he said handing her his new business card. "I don't care what I am doing. I'll stop just to run to your aid. Big Facts," he said sliding in between the suicide doors. "Take care."

"You too," she whispered softly staring deep within his eyes. He pulled from the curve as Future and Drake's newest music kicked to life.

Chapter 12

Jade and Carla started spending more time together the following months, traveling coast to coast like an artist on tour crashing all the exotic places. One week ago, they were spotted on the shores of Malibu in bright colorful bikinis. Jade knew how to market her team...by making herself the star of attraction. Carla on the other hand was just enjoying the events as they unfolded. However, this weekend would be a little different due to A&T Homecoming in Greensboro, North Carolina.

Jade knew Rick Ross, Future, Cardi B, Glorilla, Lil Baby, and more would attract bawses from all over the globe.

Jade pushed her newest volcano colored McLaren down the crowded streets slowly as her instincts had been precise. All the dope boys and celebrities were out showing off in their foreign whips. Box and Bubble Chevys were sitting high like skyscrapers on twenty-sixes with rainbow coating. Dozens of high end vehicles blazed their audio systems loudly as the sound literally deactivated all traffic.

The hustlers sported their custom outfits with designer labels, holding court with their entourage of shooters it seemed. Jade and Carla were well aware that the event created a significant amount of money hustlers spent on their intimate, platonic, business or personal relationships to impress them.

Full blooded, supremely independent, brainy, force females with unique qualities made their presence known in their Christian Louboutin, Dolce & Gabbana, Fendi, Gucci,

Dior and Saint Laurent labels. Jade felt as though she was cruising through a zoo where wild beasts of the field roamed, scrutinizing the tantalizing women who had come out lurking rapidly seeking to capture a remarkable man, with deep pockets. Although her nature expressed power, she was audacious and intent on getting her way. She welcomed the competition and was more eager to treat her opposition as an annoyance to be brushed out of the way.

Clad in self-confidence, a touch recklessness, Dior oversized shades to highlight their movie star special magnetism, Jade and Carla's supreme qualities of optimism attracted charming companions interested and interesting.

"Bitch it's on tonight. Let's get to the money." She started with an intense drive to succeed.

Young Jeezy had also performed that night and now stood on High Point Road strip accompanied by acquaintances known to most as Ceelo, Malik, and Zulu, which was a rare for him. Malik stood nearby dressed down in Balmain with a diamond chain and bracelet. While Ceelo rocked a silver and blue headband combined with a silver and blue sweater made by Balenciaga. Groupies flirtatiously flocked around the hood figures with gentleman qualities expecting to be pursued, wooed, and put into the mood.

As Jade gilded her spacecraft into a parking space, she noticed some eye candy with rare charisma, lounging in a Maybach. " He has the potential to be the perfect playmate but only if I find the game worth playing." She started with great generosity and enthusiasm. "I'm in need of a true soul companion who can share my sense of adventure.

" I need a change as well," Carla stated knowing Jade was about to put his neck into a yoke. "I'ma take his partner," she suggested pointing towards a similar Maybach his partner owned.

Carla began seeking to explore the possibilities to the fullest. She and Jade shared an idealism about men with deep pockets, love and life. However, Carla was an extravagant romantic, but very private, restrained, and aloof.

"I'm 'bout to go strike a conversation and see what's on his mind," Jade said as she slid from the carbon fiber seats onto the pavement with high aspirations. She activated the alarm from her key and both glowing highly social creatures maneuvered their way towards the possibilities of a developing affair.

"Excuse me, beautiful. You walk so sure of yourself. You walk like you the only real queen left!" The club promoter yelled from the inside of his Maybach. To him, physical desire is a necessary part of relationships.

Intrigued by his frank, earthly approach, she smiled, calculating whether he was worth her attention. "I am sure of myself. I am a queen, the center from which all others radiate."

"What's your name beautiful?"

"Jade." She started with great strength. "And yours?"

"Free Bands." He started giving her insight on how he lived. "I must admit, you have a royal quality, a way of standing out in a crowd. The unique combination of excitement you project, your sense of style, and your way of speaking, drew me to you," he said with intense feelings.

Jade was unaware that Free Bands had been watching her from a distance conversing with Malik and Ceelo inside the coliseum.

This hindered him from approaching her, but now it was now or never.

"That's interesting. I like a man who takes action instead of sitting around pondering what could be a great opportunity."

Sensing the opportunity had presented itself, he casually continued to mention his true feelings. "I see why people like to be around you. You're interesting and amusing."

"That's so true! So, where are you from Free Bands?"

"Winston Salem," he said with confidence. And you?"

"Durham."

"Yeah, I can tell you from Bull City."

"Why you say that?"

"By the way you put out your chin and walk head-on into any challenge." He started being funny, but serious at the same time. "You have a deep-seated need to prove your worth. Not to others but to yourself."

"You funny, but it's true. People dislike me because of my king-size ego."

Jade and Free Bands continued their casual conversation, which led to them continuing conversing over the phone with heart to heart talks for hours. They both enjoyed the flirtations and maneuvers of the new developing affair. Free Bands liked her charming, easy going manner and her acceptance of what the streets are like.

Due to his rare charisma, she changed herself to fit the image that Free Bands wanted. Yet, this woman of a thousand faces remained uniquely herself: elusive, untouchable, and mysterious. She had a fascination that no one quite understood.

Free Bands was actually a poor choice for what she was looking for in a companion due to his immature belief system. He liked nothing better than the chase. As Drake raps, "When he's not near the girl he loves, he loves the girl he's near." He was perfectly sincere when he told the other woman the same thing the next night. Whatever he believed at that moment was true. This is not because he has an insatiable sexual desire, but because courting a woman to him was an elusive adventure, an unexplored path. He was nothing more than the archetypal footloose and fancy-free wise street bawse searching for his feminine ideal.

However unconventional Jade's attitude may be, and however flirtatious she may seem, a man will have to convince her that she's not simply his target for tonight. He cannot make the mistake of treating her as a sex object. She expected to be courted, and a man should not press matters to a conclusion until he knows more about her than her telephone number.

Passion was not important to her; communication and money was. Jade saw men as an individual first and a bed partner second.

The moment his lips grazed hers, it was as if he was in captivity; tunnel visioned into a whirlwind of eternal bliss. Several months into their developing affair and it was still as if he was laying eyes on her for the first time, smitten and swooned; astounded by her presence as he basked in the ambience of her natural beauty.

In a standstill of anticipation, he was yearning that opening night when he would be able to have her in its entirety, because she was unlike anyone he had ever met. Being that his dream woman stood directly in front of him, he refused to let her out of his sights. Even during those times she'd play hard to get as if keeping her pussy on quarantine.

She continuously imagined him doing things to her no other dope boy had ever done. Free Bands possessed a strange sense of power that held her paralyzed with the freakiest feeling she had ever felt before. Enduring the suspense, she decided it was time to let go and initiate what they both wanted from the first glance...and soon.

***

The following night at Asia's birthday bash, Jade showed up dressed to impress, bringing sunshine into the lives of all those in attendance. She wore a remarkably Valentine red fur coat, red snakeskin leather pants, and blooded Christian Louboutin heels. Her Fendi shades sat atop her head, giving her a distinct look of a model any designer would have been pleased with. Her only wish was to be the jewel in the center of any setting.

"Hey girl, you just in time," Asia said with excitement as she welcomed Jade into her new mini mansion. "Everyone is on the courtyard patio by the pool. Malik was just about to make a toast."

"Without me. I don't believe he would do that."

"Malik just said it wouldn't be right to make a toast without the one who made it possible," she mentioned as she sauntered her way into the spacious living room. She was amazed at the soaring ceilings and walls of glass that looked to a breathtaking panoramic downtown of Charlotte, North Carolina.

"Oh my god, girl. This is a large residence. I gotta give it to you, you got hella taste." She started passing the main floor master.

"This is what I do for a hobby. Design homes."

"My intellectual friends. Jade has finally arrived." Malik started getting everyone's attention.

"Hello, my truest of truest friends," she stated wearing a Mona Lisa. "The goddess of love and beauty is here to bring out smiles," she boasted expecting admiration.

"You look amazing," Castro stated as the two embraced sharing real love. "How was your trip to the mountains?"

"It was great actually. I needed that time alone," she stated with strong passion that sparked Castro's mind. He needed a trip away as well. But time never would allow that to happen. "Where Free?"

"In the entertainment room," he shared as his eyes followed those of Notorious. "Let me get back with you."

"Boy bye," she stated as she sashayed her way in the opposite direction.

"Asia, where did you get that diamond watch from?" She was fascinated by the things money can buy.

"It's a gift from Malik."

"Oh, I'm jealous bitch." Jade admitted swiftly.

"Don't be, sweetheart. Your friendships and associations bring opportunities for all of us. I'm delighted to be a part of the winning circle." Asia shared with great passion. "By the way, I love that fur coat. Where did you get that from?"

"A couple of weeks ago, Free went to Philly with me to visit my father in prison, and gifted me with three colorful minks."

"At least he is spending time with you. Malik is always on the track. But hopefully things will get better now that we are in Charlotte. I want to travel, and see the world with my man."

"And in due time you will. Malik trying to get that bread in loaves."

"I understand that. I'm just really venting right now. We good though."

"Well that's all that matters, because it could be worse."

"Facts," Asia said, giving her insight of her truest words. "This may sound old fashioned, but Malik is the man of my dreams. He's a romantic daydreamer who loves beautiful things and I understand and respect that. I just work on myself by making our home a place my man never wants to leave."

"Well said," Jade said as she noticed Free Bands coming her way.

"Hi beautiful," Free said, folding her into his arms.

"Why you just now pulling up," she whispered in a way he could only hear.

"Did you put the kegal inside your pussy?"

"Yes, I can't believe you talked me into doing this." She laughed.

"We got this. Just realize, have a lot of drinks and enjoy the moment. We making history today because of your vision."

"That's why I adore you."

"Whatever," he said with strong emotions.

"Don't whatever me."

"Whatever." He leaned to kiss her.

Jade moaned as he continued to bite on her neck causing a tingling sensation through her body. "Don't do that. This kegal got me horny. What are you doing to me?" She said spinning on her heels into his arms kissing him on the lips.

Moments later, after Glorilla finished performing in honor of Asia, they all toasted to her happiness. She was definitely enjoying her birthday bash as the tears streamed from her sensual eyes, as she opened the last of many presents.

Turning to face her passionate bed partner. "Bae, I love you forever, because you bring out the best in me. Big facts," she said with a secure sense of her own judgment.

Malik then grabbed her by the hand with a gentle squeeze of affection and led the brightest star in heaven out to the deck, leading to the garage where she spotted an attractive Bentley coupe with a red bow on it.

Asia was speechless as she bolted down the steps towards the Continental GT V8 First Edition. She was elated with happiness as she opened the driver side door and fell onto the soft seats. "Malik, I never expected this even though you did promise me one. Bae, you did that."

"I just want the woman of my dreams to share my dreams with me. I told you; you were going to be the first real chick to come through in a Bentley. How you going to attract millionaire clients if you ain't pulling up in something foreign?"

Once back inside, they conversed amongst one another sipping on expensive champagne, smoking large blunts, laughing and sharing casual conversations about building a brighter future. Thus far, the night was a world series. Spirits were transforming into lovely love as their emotions were derived from Chris Brown's song Warm Embrace sparked the interest of passion between these matched partners.

"So, tell me a little about yourself." Destiny asked Lucky as she eyed Malik dancing romantically with the woman that catered to his every whim. For right now, she had to keep her passions for him on tight rein, but underneath her emotions were moving in waves.

Though she may not show it, this woman cares a great deal about love. Deep within, she is an extravagant diva, but very private. She is very discerning when it comes to her special assignments. She has no time to waste with the help. Getting what she needed done mattered more to her. If a dope boy doesn't measure up like Lucky, she uses him like a pawn. If a dope boy interests her, she will watch him like a hawk from an emotional distance before moving closer. She takes the time to observe him and considers carefully the consequences of her involvement.

In the front master bedroom, light sounds of mumbling could be heard as Destiny and Lucky stood nearby the stairway. Without warning, Lucky opened the door noticing Notorious on her knees giving Castro some super head. She turned to face Lucky with dead presidents on her agenda and said, "If you come in, come in, but please shut that door and continued caressing Castro's huge black cock until her client was fully satisfied.

Moments later, the two animals exited the room and headed back to the spacious living room. Castro appeared first unnoticed. Notorious followed only seconds later. With animal-like characteristics, no one noticed their absence nor their return.

Around 2 a.m., Jade sauntered her way towards Free, tipsy and ready to leave. He informed her that he would be ready in a minute. He was seriously entangled in a real cash game of monopoly. And right now he was losing close to a hundred bands.

And he was very close to losing a hundred bands. Moments later, the game ended in Malik's favor. After the Lebron handshakes, everyone hopped into their individual push starts, dashing in the night fog with deep sexual demands in motion. For Jade, the last meal had just been served. Her taste buds were in the prowl for something savory; something a lot more alluring and delicious. Clenching onto every reflection of her imagination, urging her into an intoxicating state of lustful bliss, in anticipation of their union becoming a tangible reality.

Sexual fantasies constantly traveled through her imagination. Rampantly running wild at times leaving her mind vacant of all knowledge needed to properly articulate herself. But the pure essence of its being regarding their mental bond that they shared captivated her thought process. Almost making it unbearable to fight the craving of wanting to explore every inch of Free Bands banana; longing for the feeling of pinnacle passion within their loving making scenario as they finally united as one. Soft music played as they shared orgasm after orgasm devouring one another way into the early morning, which left both animals feeling completely exhausted.

Malik and Asia arrived in Saint Thomas for the Christmas holiday from college. However, it was more like a vacation rather than a break from school. The Virgin Islands was framed by luxurious ocean views and condos. Asia was elated with joy as she witnessed the bastion wall, terraced fountains and working water cannons at the Waterfront Estate. Asia was surprised when Malik informed her he had purchased the condo they were staying in.

"So this you?" Asia asked wanting to know more.

"Nah, ain't no I in team. This us. I said as I grow, we grow," he assured her as he kissed her on the top of her forehead. "Now, when you need some down time, or just feel like vacating with your friends, you can bring them here."

She raised her head and with a sensual look in her eyes. She said, "This was definitely a good investment." She caressed his chest.

Upon laying her head on his chest she began to reflect. She couldn't believe she'd graduated from high school and now lived in a mini mansion and drove a Bentley. Now, her eyes were set on law school, and eventually get married.

"You alright?" Malik asked after noticing Asia in deep thought.

"Yeah, I'm fine." She shot back.

"Regardless of what I may think or say, let me know what's going on because I care."

She maintained silent, not quite knowing how to express herself.

"Baby, I worry about you more now than I ever have. I can't sleep at night and when I do sleep I have nightmares.

I just don't want to see you get messed up cause you a good man. My man at that," she confessed sitting up to face him in bed.

"Bae, nothing is going to happen to me. I choose my steps more wisely now; I'm learning the ground," he expressed choosing his words carefully. "And besides, I got the best lawyers to represent me if shit was to go left."

"And who may that be?" She asked suddenly.

"Bill Thomas and you." He smiled.

"Facts. Bill is good, but I haven't even taken the bar exam yet."

"Facts, but you have taken the first step without seeing the entire pathway. In my eyes, you the feminine Johnny Cochran."

"Thanks for believing in me, but seriously, the feds could be watching you. How many young guys from the hood going to UNC and driving a Bentley?"

"You gotta point. But I'm not just any dude. I'm the best thing since Jordan, so it's nothing for me to have and drive what I want. I'm just a small pawn in this complex game of high chance and stakes. My seasonal time on the track is coming to a place of completion. I came, I saw, and conquered."

"I'm sure you mean well, but that's something you can't promise. One thing for certain with the feds, when they watch you, a secret indictment can come years later. They're so cunning they only come when you least expect it."

"That's why I'ma do what's been presented to me and walk away a richer man with no stain on my shirt."

"That's the goal, but I'm sure that's every drug dealer's dream. But it doesn't always end that way.

Do what you gotta do, but at the same time be careful. I'm with you regardless of the outcome. Big facts," he stated as she leaned over to kiss him.

Moments later, they were making slow delicious love in ways they had never experienced from the bed to the rooftop deck, finishing in the shower only to end up back in bed unsatisfied. Six orgasms later, they drifted off to sleep, embraced in each other's arms.

When the early morning hours arrived, Malik rose and went outside to enjoy the uninterrupted view of the ocean and falls from the cliff side pool.

"Mmmmmmmmmm...good morning daddy!" Asia whispered softly embracing him from behind. "You up mighty early."

"I couldn't help it. The view of the ocean is beautiful. I couldn't possibly sleep through moments like this. The city is never this relaxing. This place gives me a distinct feeling that's insurmountable and an incredible sense of satisfaction."

"Well, I'm glad you're enjoying yourself. You needed this time to reflect on your life, where it is and where you trying to go," she stated as a true friend and lover.

"Damn...I could stay out here for a lifetime, listening to the soundtrack of the ocean," he expressed this as he watched a couple jog along the beach. "Whatcha think about that?"

"That would be nice, but would you really give up everything for this?" She responded, hoping he would answer this question truthfully.

"Facts. As soon as I handle this one last move," he said as Kream's words reminded him of the vision. "I want to spend the best of my sunsets with you."

"Remember now, promises are easy to make, but hard to deliver," she whispered. "But I'ma hold you to that promise. I'm about to go shower, wanna join me?"

"Of course...why not," he stated. Suddenly, they both dashed toward the stunning master bath at high speed.

Upon reaching their destination they exploded in laughter. "You cheated," Asia said coming up the rear.

Malik spun around to face Asia and said, "I'll make it up to you."

They both stared at each with lust in their eyes. Asia slowly walked towards him, dropping her gown to the floor, as radiating heat evaporated from her skin. Before Malik could react, she leaped into his arms wrapping her legs around his waist smiling.

"Daddy, take me right here in the wall." She gasped, breathing heavily as Malik slammed her back to wall. "Uhhh..."

She grunted as his aggressive behavior turned her on as she felt him fill her insides without delay. She smothered his mouth with her full soft lips as they slithered each other's tongue. The feeling of his tongue exploring her mouth created a vacuum of excitement in Asia that she had never known before. An electrifying shock instantly thundered throughout her erecting her nipples to razor stiffness. "Ooohh." She grasped, pulling her lips from his.

As Malik slid his hands down caressing the soft flesh of her breast with his skillful touch heightening her desire, Asia moaned in delight as he began flickering his tongue ravishly like a newborn thirsty for milk. Dimly aware of his hand lightly caressing her vagina, she gasped from the deriving sensation tingling through her body.

He eased his index finger gently inside her deep causing her to arch her back automatically, working in a circular motion. Breathing became heavy as she smeared her juices around her vagina like hot oil. "Your so fucking wet," he said dropping his boxers to the floor, crumbling around his ankles. As Asia rested on his thighs, he carefully lifted his feet out of them, kicking them off to the side. Pulling his finger out, he spread her inner lips exposing her clitoris.

"Ooooh..." She grasped as he lightly grazed it with a set finger, as she was unable to withstand it any longer. She reached down and grabbed his swollen black cock and placed the organ against her entrance.

"Ssssss..." She hissed through clenched teeth. "Oh...Oh...fuck me harder tonight daddy, mmmm," she said softly, moaning.

"Let's have a baby in St. Thomas," He gladly stated, entering her with a massive hard on, reaching her pelvis with one thrust.

"Aaaa..." She cried out gasping for air.

"Yes...Yes...Yes...fuck me, deeper..." She whispered in his ear as she squeezed his arms tightly.

"Deeper.. Deeper...Right there..." she moaned. "Ah, this dick is so fucking good...sss...shit, damn you a beast," she said with the look of fear in her eyes and pleasure reaping in her body.

"Who's pussy is this?" He asked, thrusting her slowly.

"Oh...Ohh,..its alllllll yours Malik Carter, Aka, Kream. All yours...right there, Kream. Don't stop," she said rising to meet each stroke with a graceful motion. "I'm 'bout to cum all over your dick...Oh fuck," she whispered making facial expressions to exemplify the pleasure of being loved. " Cum with me...Oh, Oh." She yelled desperately grasping to catch her breath.

As the intensity raised, and the moans grew louder, Kream began to pound each thrust to the hilt, bringing Asia closer and closer to climax. Suddenly, in a swift motion, Kream moaned, making wild life animal sounds, as he slammed his huge black cock into her clutching her ass cheeks together driving his banana deeper and deeper into her pounding massive thrusts violently as they both exploded together screaming satisfied and content.

Kream rolled off of Asia and drew her closer to him, "Baby, I love you," he stated reflecting on how she had been with him through all the stormy weather. "Our love will always have purpose for us to always stay together. You my forever.."

"And I'm forever yours," she replied with an understanding smile.

As "Moments" by Rajan feat. Sahra played softly in their ears, they continued to whisper words of love and fidelity until they drifted off to sleep, together. And when she awoke, he was still there.

That night they walked the beach and enjoyed themselves at the Casino after spending a major amount of time gambling. Having fun spending quality time together meant the most, as they would always cherish the moment for years to come.

At one boutique, Asia dumped like ten bands on a variety of toys and lingerie to tease and please Kream. At another, Kream splurged on more gifts for his Princess, dumping close to thirty bands on the counter. As they exited, they drew more attention to themselves with armful of Christian Dior bags.

They spent an enormous amount of money as they ventured throughout the island as if they were the island's richest inclined couple. They stayed constantly in each other's presence the entire vacation as they fashioned each moment strictly for them and their followers. Jade fed the streets leaving him with no worries. His focus was on pleasing his woman and masterminding his next move.

The trip was just what he needed.

The last day in The Virgin Islands, Kream and Asia enjoyed a pleasingly quiet dinner on the sandy beach surrounded by tropical foliage and coconut groves. The food was immaculate as they drank expensive brands of champagne as Kehlani performed Love Language live. They partied into the night, cultivating each other's mind and learning each other's desires as they conversed. The champagne stirred emotions upon Asia as she down six shots in a row. Suddenly, feeling sexually attached to him, she expressed her desire for him to make love to her one more time before they return home, to a place of distractions. She was now tipsy, which provocatively inspired her to engage in wet ass pussy conversation.

"Please take me some place, any place, and make soft, sweet, love to me," she whispered softly, across the candlelit table laced with sensuous lust.

"Repeat that."

"Soft, slow, and exquisite," she said, running her fingers through her hair.

"Oh really. Where would you like to film this erotic movie?" He said feeling the vibe of the emotions she expressed.

"We could rent a yacht and sail to the middle of the ocean, and let the cool breeze dance over our bodies until sunrise."

Aware that she desperately wanted to fulfill one of her dreams, he leaned across the table with his lips only inches away from hers and said, "Let's make it happen tonight." Instantly, he gently kissed her.

She kissed him back. Without hesitation they both stood to their feet. Kream left a pleasant tab as they made their way to a rented Super Sprinter awaiting them out front. As they entered the Mercedes, Asia slouched morosely in the high quality leather seat as the theater sound system, larger front and rear Smart TV came to life. "I need to handle something. I'll be right back."

"1 thought we were going to spend every moment together," she asks, puzzled.

"We are. I just need to handle one last thing. Trust me, this will be a night to remember," he whispered before placing a sloppy kiss on her cheek.

Once Kream returned, he instructed the driver with instructions to his next destination to complete his task.

Complying with his demands, the chauffeur slowly pulled away masking a smile that Kream could not foresee. However, the night was a success.

Kream and Asia arrived back at Charlotte the following day where Asia's girlfriend, Kendra met them at the airport, driving them home. The moment Kream entered his domain, he stripped down and went into the bathroom. He ran the shower until it was pleasantly warm, then let the water cascade down his back for at least seven minutes. He soaped himself in Dove, before climbing out of the shower and later went to sleep, while Asia shared details of their trip to her best friend of seventeen years.

The next morning, Kream woke and fixed him a bowl of Berry Colossal Cereal before informing Asia that he had to make a quick run but promised to return sometime later. However, Asia was too exhausted to respond.

Kream pulled out of his driveway in dashing SC500 headed to Durham as music by Future filtered through the sound system. Having called Jade two hours ago, Kream stopped by her mother's house spotting her standing in the yard. Jade slowly approached the two seated coupe and climbed in the passenger of the Lexus.

Kream quickly looked her over, and as usual she was beautiful as ever dressed snugly in Chanel.

"Red Rum Salute," he said as she closed the door. "I miss you like crazy. Big Facts."

"Red Rum Salute gang. The feelings are mutual," she stated looking him over. "I'm tired as hell. Me, Ceelo, Carla, and Snatch flew down to Atlanta for New Years, and partied like rock stars. But for some reason it just wasn't the same without you," he said fiddling with her phone. "Your presence always makes a difference."

"Well I'm back now, and as a friend you have my undivided attention."

"Thanks, I needed to hear that," he spoke truthfully with a smile.

She then brought him up to date on the day to day grind on the track she had conducted while he was away. She also informed him of the fresh ten bricks she picked up this morning. Kream smiled knowing she had conducted herself satisfactorily as he knew she would.

"So how was your vacation?" She asked.

"Heaven on earth. We had a great time. We hung out on the beach, went shopping, played games at the casino, and danced at the jazz club. I even surprised her with a private personalized cruise on the yacht."

"Boy bye," Jade replied with excitement.

"No cap. We took a cruise on a rented yacht. The night life on the water is beautiful," Kream replied in amazement. "How was your trip to the mountains?"

"Much needed. I needed some down time to recuperate," she replied half truthfully.

Although she did travel down to Tennessee to recuperate, her main reason was to meet with a potential connect named Teflon. Teflon was a member of a California gang under the Mexican Mafia called 18 St. The two had met one weekend while visiting a friend in Maryland. Teflon was a big face in the streets with great passions for wealth. Jade was an opportunity for him in money ways only. With her persistence and his rational approach made a good money making combination, so they made arrangements to meet Tennessee a month later.

"How you and Free?" He replied changing the subject.

"I haven't spoken to him in weeks."

"Why, what happened?" Kream asked, wanting to know more. "He really likes you."

"That's what I am afraid of. I am not the one to make the best of a bad bargain," she replied showing no interest in Free at all. "If I am unhappy, I won't resign myself or compromise or try to work things out. I'll just walk away."

"You cold."

"No. I just don't take love as seriously as most women. Besides, Free doesn't measure up."

Malik had very high standards, so Jade knew if she decided to fuck with Free Bands, he had to be willing to measure up to Malik's standards. Jade knew the facts. Malik was the undisputed truth. She never knew another man that thoroughly. Malik in her eyes was a Lion, the King of the streets, one who gave the streets an impression of being in firm control of his next move like a true predator on the prowl in search of his next meal.

"But he has potential, and I don't think you should let him go."

"Why?" She asked puzzled by his request.

"Because we may need him to stretch out brand. I would love to send a few homies down to Winston Salem to set up shop. So, I need to think outside the box for me. Matter fact call him now."

Malik. Please, not now."

"No, right now," he replied with slight pressure.

Jade phoned Free Bands. He was delighted to hear her voice, even though she had given him the most abrupt and hurtful brush off several weeks ago.

"I'm trying to come see you. Can I pull up?" She asked sweetly.

He was hesitant at first, but realized he had started to forget how bad she had hurt him.

When and where? " he questioned.

"I don't know. Maybe this weekend. You've been on my mind so I want to see you."

"How about Thursday?"

"I'm actually free tomorrow."

"Well, tomorrow it is."

"See you then." She pressed to end the call, and looked at Malik, who stood by her side. "Satisfied?"

"Of course. He's happy and I'm happy."

"He did sound excited. That's for sure."

"I knew he couldn't neglect you."

"No man can neglect this woman. But no cap, I really did not want to call him." She turned to face Malik. "Do I really have to see him?"

"Only until I figure things out. You can handle it. You a big girl. If it doesn't make dollars, it doesn't make sense."

"That's why I love you Malik. You always look out for my best interest." She hugged him.

"I do what I do for the team. Let's get this money."

The next day, Free Bands had Jade meet her at the arena in Charlotte to watch The Hornets versus The Brooklyn Nets play. Afterward, he wanted to surprise her, and he drove his Maserati to Charlotte to his condos. He had obviously been there earlier in the day because the table was laid for two, with candles waiting to be lit and two chefs cooking in front of them.

"Surprise!" He said. "I wanted this night to be special. I thought it would be nice if we were alone since we always seem to be surrounded by your friends." Moments later, he was all over her. "Jade, I'm really feeling you. But at the same time you hurt me when you stop taking my calls for no reason. Now that we are trying to work things out. I want us to look for a house together, get engaged and hopefully be married in a year." He reached into his pocket and produced a jewelry box. "This is for you. I just want you to know that I love you, Jade. I always have, and always will." He plunged his mouth down on hers, kissing her frantically.

Malik had not instructed her how to handle this love and romance situation. But she knew she had to play the game so Malik could use his influence to open up the floodgates of attracting clientele in Winston Salem. So, although she didn't feel like it, she kissed him back, and let his hands linger for a moment on her breast before pushing him away.

"Not right, now Free," she told him sharply.

"I understand Cupcake. You know how I am when it comes to you."

Idly, she glanced at the diamond ring he had presented her with. It was beautiful. She removed it from the box and slipped it on her finger. It fit perfectly. To make him happy, she decided to wear it for now...but give it back to him when Malik did what he promised to do.

"Do you like it?" Free asked anxiously.

"I love it Free."

"You're the most attractive woman I ever seen." He grabbed her by the waist, exploring her mouth with his tongue, allowing his hands to slip from her waist to her ass.

It spite of herself, she felt excited. He wanted her so badly that she couldn't help feeling the surge of power. How surprised he would be if he knew the facts. She had noticed the bulge in his jeans, and that gave her a feeling of power also.

"Have you been seeing anyone since our last encounter?" She asked, pushing him away once more, and watching him to gauge his reaction.

"Not at all," he said, flushing.

That's why we can't be together," she replied. "You lying and you know it."

He looked up from his phone. "Jay, you can't be serious right now."

"I'm dead ass. How do you expect us to be engaged, if you gotta lie to me? She teased. Tell me everything, regardless of how I may feel."

"Yeah, I am seeing someone but it ain't that serious. She just a temporary thrill. What I want is in front of me."

Jade wanted to laugh in his face. How young and naive and romantic his words were. Free Bands had a lot to learn and Jade was just the right woman to teach the baby.

***

"You been doing a lot of back and forth to Free's spot later," he mentioned as he laid on his bed at the Marriott Hotel in Cary. "Let me find out he got you in a yoke."

Jade grinned back as she stood beside the bed. "I can't help he finds me irresistible."

"Come lay down." He patted a space beside him. "Let's pillow talk."

"I wish I could, but I need to go home and pack. Free taking me to Miami for the weekend."

"Really. It seems like since the two of you back talking, you don't have time to chill with me."

"Malik! I'm doing this for us. Remember...you were the one who said I needed to concentrate on Free."

Malik raised his eyebrows. He did make that play, but he didn't expect her to fall back in love. He had imagined she would come running for him, unable to wait to leap into his bed. Actually, he really did not want to sleep with her, but he had steeled himself to the fact that he had to at least once. However, since Free had been making progress, she obviously did not want to sleep with Malik. Was the finesser losing his finesse?

Suddenly, he began to sink in his feelings. "Look, are you sure you can handle your role without getting too emotionally involved?"

Jade paid him no mind, showering his face with ten thousand kisses. "Malik, really? I got this one in the bag." Secretly, she was thrilled, because Malik seemed a bit jealous.

"I trust you. I just miss our time together," he said. "So, what information do you have for me?"

"Well, let me see." She paused provocatively, enjoying her small moment of power. "He moved that dog food for sure."

"What he playing with?"

"At least three, but he's just the face. His brother put in the foot work."

"I see you have done your homework well."

"I try to please. When should I approach him on a business proposition?"

Give it like another month."

"I guess."

Malik sat thoughtfully on the side of the bed. For Jade, it was just playing games. She believed in his dream; she just didn't realize that she had to connect all the dots in order for the dream to become a reality. But if she wanted him and all the promises he had made, she would have to pay for the privilege. And she would. Malik would make sure of that.

Chapter 14

A week later, Malik prepared to conduct a transaction with Free Bands. He had agreed to buy three bricks and Malik would front the other three on consignment. Jade promised to deliver them to him. Malik had ten more to get rid of before Ceelo received the next shipment of one hundred bricks of dog food. His plans were to bring his vision into an existing reality. With so much money, a few foreign whips, house and a Michelle Obama by his side, he figured it would be best to fall back after his last run. Asia had raised a valid point while on vacation, and now he felt the slight possibility that the Feds could be watching him and his crew.

"Bruh, it's time we aim for Big Meech status and run it up. I got a play set up and with a world class performance we could walk away with outstanding results." Kream started trying to get Malik to see his next play as a chance to enhance his kingdom. "I fully understand Asia's point, but we can't hold on to those negative images. There's no need for us to run through these streets now with psychological emergency brakes on. We here now. It's our time to run it up," Kream mentioned motivating himself.

Although Malik did consider falling back just to see if the Feds were watching, a part of him wanted to push down harder on the gas and move toward his ultimate destiny, so he continued to listen.

"There's a lot of potential in this opportunity. And if we give it all we got we know that what we seek and expect, we will find. We live in a strange and fast-paced world, and though each day the world we live in is being altered by beasts like us who have learned to unlock their unborn creativity in the game of a cut throat, we must greet every interaction with animal instincts. Kill or be killed," Kream whispered knowing he was now on his way to becoming the first hood billionaire.

It was only a matter of time before he would make his next move his best move like Lebron James to the paint on all contenders who wanted to compete against him.

"The number one problem that keeps people from winning in the streets in lack of belief in themselves, their team, and their vision. You get what you expect. I'm just trying to strengthen your subconscious but you gotta believe in the vision first, then yourself, and go for it. We deserve to be on top bruh, because we know how to finesse the finesser and call the right shots. Are you in or what?"

Kream started setting the tone for his vision to feel more attainable.

"Malik!" Asia yelled for the second time. "Why are you standing in front of the mirror talking to yourself?" She asked him standing before the threshold of the bathroom door.

Malik turned to face her with a look of determination in his eyes. Asia had no clue that the man she now saw and spoke to in the mirror was his alter ego, and the two had been conversing in great depth concerning their life and future plans.

"I'm good," he responded looking at her as she stood before him in a camisole and thong.

"Just got a lot on my plate right now...But you good though?" He asked shutting the water off.

"I guess," she chimed in, bothered by the fact she had never seen the man she saw in Malik moments ago. "I thought I heard you talking to someone, so I came to be nosey."

"Well nosey your way back into your law books." He started turning to face her.

"You need to be doing something. Don't you have an Ethics paper to write?"

"Facts. I'm on it. You better believe that" he stated with excitement. "Why Kream?" Malik asked, smiling winningly.

"Because you always make me Kream on that dick," she replied , returning the smile.

They continued to converse while concerning a couple of issues. After dressing, he left to meet up with his crew. The day quickly passed as they conducted business through each trap house with strict gangster affiliation, collecting more than a quarter million in cash, and five thousand in clothing.

Malik tossed and turned that night in bed unable to sleep as he kept visualizing himself as the "Dope King" with enormous racks. Pondering the thought of how he was going to make a billion dollars as Kream had mentioned, knowing frustrations came with making money at this level. The problem was he had six million ways he could spend a few million. But in order to live the dream he had to attract big people, and at the rate he had been climbing it felt like it would take forever, having to hand half of what he made to Ceelo, and share the rest of the profits with Jade, Castro, Snatch and Hysheem. He struggled with his options as he tried to will himself to sleep weighing the pros and the cons of the game.

He was not afraid of the dangers of the street life; he was more afraid of someone in his circle ratting him out if things were to go sour knowing strong men go down like that. He knew the feds had ways of turning friends against their leaders. The solution came to him that night as his excitement grew he could hardly contain his impatience, but he knew he had to until he spoke with Hysheem with a preamble.

Weeks passed as he constantly racked in money with blurring speed. The remaining kilos of dog food had sold swiftly. During that time, all he did was make plays before and after classes and on weekends. Out of twenty four hours a day, he was only sleeping four, being that there was money in the city to be made. Snatch, Castro, Hysheem and Jade handled each individual trap while Malik attended classes during the day. They were all loyal to him with no questions asked or any problems. The money flowed fluently. Every so often, he would sacrifice all play and business to spend time with his crew members individually.

One Saturday morning, Malik and Hysheem played a few games of chess attempting to pick his brain and allowing him to examine himself. Together they had been playing for the last three hours at five thousand dollars a game. The score was tied up at a game apiece as they sat before enormous size plasma in the entertainment room blazing gas.

"Never leave the help in the cold," Malik warned taking Hysheem's pawn with his rook. "Especially if he's keeping you warm with his life."

"I didn't think you were watching that side of the board." He smiled. "Check!" There was a moment of silence as Malik planned his next move. "In most cases you right, but there comes a time when you must sacrifice your weakest man in order to draw out the enemy's strongest man."

Malik looked dumbfounded by Hysheem's desperate but cautious move. With penetrating eyes, Malik examined the board carefully, "That was a good move my nigga," he replied, moving his King out of the fear of danger. He then pulled hard on his blunt.

"So, how's your lil man?" He asked Hysheem.

"He growing that's for sure." He smiled.

"That's what's up. How's his mother?" He asked, moving a piece for protection towards his knight. "She good?"

"Facts. You know I keep her sauced in the latest fashion."

"That's what it's about. Making sure the family is good."

"Big Facts." Agreed Hysheem. We living, homie."

"Facts, but we just getting started." Exclaimed Malik. "Look, I can't go into full detail right now, but we about to run it up so I'ma need you to stay focused and solid. I can handle the rest."

"Say less."

"We don't have any room for error." Demanded Kream. "Are we clear?"

"No question..." Hysheem said. "You know I stay on demon time."

Malik was not sure if he wanted to bring him in on his unaccompanied mission, but he knew at some point he would have to trust him since there was no one else he could trust to pull off such a plan of action.

"Bruh, let me ask you something," he said, pondering his words carefully. "Do you move in the street like you do chess?"

"Everything I do is well thought out." Hysheem exclaimed. "I just don't move to be moving."

Interrupted by his phone jangling on the table, he answered without looking at the caller ID. "Who dis?"

"What's popping homie? Where you at?" Castro asked.

"Sitting here playing chess with Hysheem. Why, what's good?"

"I need for you to come pick me up. I'm at Joel's friend's house. My car ready. They just called me like twenty minutes ago."

"Aight, give me a second. Text me the address," he stated before ending the call.

With one swift motion, Malik and Hysheem grabbed the North Face coats, headed towards the garage and climbed into Malik's Lexus. They sprang away with surprising speed. Moments later, after dropping Hysheem off, Malik pulled alongside the curve in front of Joel's condo and called his comrade, Castro.

"I'm on my way, gang. Give me one minute," Castro replied, glancing over his shoulder to Joel who was standing over by the stairway. "I'ma get at you later aight.," he said kissing her on the lips.

"Okay baby." She smiled. "You be careful."

" I have no choice. I won't be gone long," he responded by kissing her again as if he was going on a weeklong trip.

She nodded her head in agreement knowing her day would be long and lonely without Castro being away.

As Castro gradually sauntered towards Malik's Lexus, Joel stood in silence with her arms folded across her chest leaning against the door. She couldn't help releasing a flashing dazzling smile being she admired how smart, handsome, and confident he looked in his Gucci hat, jacket, and sneakers. His bowlegs was not all that bad either she thought as she closed her door and went back inside.

Only months ago, Joel awoke to the sound of the phone ringing. It was 7:45 in the morning, normally she would be awake, but lately she had been taking sleeping pills and they seemed to make it more difficult to get up in the morning.

It was Dwazha. "Have you been on the net this morning?" She demanded shrilly.

"You know I am taking a break from social media," replied Joel, already knowing where this conversation was going.

"Bitch, I told you that bitch was a bitch. So say the word, I'ma go beat that bitch ass myself."

"What bitch?" Joel questioned. She knew it would be another topic of discussion in the company of her friends. None of her friends liked Ceelo nor the grimy bitch he was with. These bitches want what you have he has continually told her. The internet is full of lies about people that matter. But Dwazha appeared to take every video on the net as gospel, and she made sure she allowed anything about her man to slip by her best friend Joel unnoticed.

"You by your phone?" Dwazha asked, focusing all her attention now to the screen of her phone. "I'm about to pull up."

She found the two videos and hit send. There were two 51 second videos of Ceelo smashing some unknown exotic flower from the back, who for a time could not tell who she was until she gazed back at him.

Joel sat on the edge of the bed and carefully examined the second video, finally realizing they had been having an affair for almost two years now. Joel was devastated and felt that her best friend, Destiny had only befriended her to get closer to her man. Now, she was walking in spiritual depression. Somewhat too embarrassed to confront Destiny or Ceelo. Eventually, she knew she would but not at the moment. She wanted to save more money, work on building enough courage to confront him, pack her things and leave. She always held some indication when he was having sex with other women, but courting her best friend was the deal breaker. She vowed to get even.

Anger, confusion, sadness, resentment, guilt, betrayal, trust, and other symptoms associated with emotional pain that accompanied her depression kept her from sleeping on lonely nights as Ceelo ran the streets, sleeping in other exotic roses sheets. The insomnia caused her to toss and turn at night. At times, she would sit in front of the TV during the wee hours of the night crying and eating all types of junk food she could to fill the void.

Weeks later, Joel began to selfheal and rebuild her broken heart. She wanted to be able to live her best life without reflecting on her past pain. Her past was just that, her past. It was time for her to love herself again. However, the only way she thought she could achieve such a challenge and receive clarity was by spending a lot of time with her new friend, Castro. They enjoyed each other's company. Their time was exactly that, their time, and their time apart was exactly that, their time apart. Even though she decided to take things slow, Castro honored her wishes with a smile. Not long afraid of many pillow talks, they soon began taking trips from coast to coast. Always enjoying themselves and the moment the universe had allowed them to share together.

One morning, Joel phoned Castro from her sister's apartment in Houston and told him that she had been sick and needed to be held. Without warning, he jumped on the plane and flew out to Texas and spent the entire weekend with her. Her sister, Janel was pleased to see Castro nurse her sister back to her best self.

On the third morning of his visit, Joel felt overly vigorous and surprised him with a full course breakfast in bed. Once she filled up his belly, she felt the need of some sexual healing. She was now ready to seduce him since she had not given up the sex the entire time they had been talking.

Until now, she only gave him enough affection to keep him, allowing him to unbutton her shirt and caress her firm breasts, but never did she let his hands stray below her waist.

Relaxing him, she began caressing and massaging him and feeding him sliced apples, while using her free hand to elevate his love muscle to its full erect capacity. Constantly rubbing her thumb over the head of his black cock until she could no longer stand it, she began sucking the pre-cum off her fingers. Wildly excited, she climbed on top of his face in a sixty-nine position unaware that Castro was the pussy eating king. He sucked her pussy and clit with the desire no other man had shown, as she steadily made tantalizing circles around his shallow banana with the tip of her tongue as she slowly dragged her lips up and down his shaft with skills only slowing to inform him she wanted him to cum in her mouth.

Sensing he was near orgasm, she hummed around his dick with vibrating sensations no other woman could match. Instead of cumming in her throat, he pulled his dick out of her mouth and flipped her on her back spreading her legs.

Once they were wide open exposing her wetness, he entered her to the hilt with one full thrust dropping his erect cock into her walls deeply. Digging his thuggish nature style and technique intensely, she wrapped her legs around his neck, grinding her pussy up towards his thick shaft contracting her vagina muscles. He pounded her pussy, fucking her hard, long and deep.

Moments later, she climaxed to the extreme before lying in bed kissing him passionately and having a heart to heart conversation until they had the energy to go another round.

"Why you smiling for?" Castro mumbled.

"Just thinking how good you make me feel," she said with affection.

Joel knew she would have never survived her restless lonely nights if Castro wouldn't have held her down through her problems with social and emotional support as a true friend, and she was so grateful for him. Castro had offered his shoulder on many occasions for her to cry on during her lonely days and nights while Ceelo slept with other women.

***

As Malik pulled away from Joel's driveway, the loving couple waved goodbye to one another.

"Bruh, ever since you been fucking with shorty, you been all out of character. Let me find out she got you open bruh," exclaimed Malik.

"You the one buying these bitches Bentley's." Castro shot back.

"You spending all this time with Jade and ain't smashed yet. What's really good with that?"

"Asia can have the world if I got something to do with it. I'm her first and last," Malik stated feeling some type of way. "As far as Jade, there's really no reason for me to rush into anything with her, because I know it'll eventually happen." He boasted proudly.

"Facts. Asia is the undisputed truth. But Jade is all over the place right now. She's obviously feeling that nigga Free;

did you see how she was all over him at the spot the other night?"

"That's all role play. I can freeze that situation whenever I want. Remember that," Malik said sharing a great zest of power and a forward looking viewpoint.

"Do you homie, because I'm definitely gonna do me."

"With who Joel?"

"Facts. I'm just waiting for her to pull the plug on Ceelo."

"She's not gone leave that nigga regardless of what he does. The money is too good," Malik said suddenly, braking for the light.

"Everyone has a story to tell, but I know the facts."

"Which is..."

"It's over for that nigga. She's done. Big facts."

"She may be, but you better be extremely careful, shorty. You do remember how you and Snatch violated her. If she ever finds out, she gon' dead you on sight. Big facts."

After a moment of silence, Castro reached into his coat pocket fishing for his box of Newport's, removing one, placing it in his mouth. "Nah, she wouldn't do that!" He replied with confidence.

"Whatever the two of you got going on doesn't sit well with me, but you are your own man," he mentioned while replaying the whole situation in his head. "Bruh, you fucking with a bitch you and your man raped. You honestly think this shit ain't gone come back and haunt you?"

Malik reflected on how far they had come since that dark night, and the truth of that matter was the game was about to change even more. He never would have thought that such a night could have set his life in motion even if someone would have forewarned him.

"It is what it is, gang. But shorty ain't showed no sign that she know shit." He shot back. "Bruh, trust me. I be on that bitch like a hawk."

"If it was me, I wouldn't be anywhere around that bitch. Bruh, she thinks about that shit every day. Be careful," Malik warned.

With penetrating eyes, Malik noticed two unmarked cars blocking both sides of the street forcing all traffic to stop between them. Castro looked around with tiger eyes attempting to read the situation as two officers stood by checking license and registration of each driver passing by their checkpoint.

"Bruh, get right," Malik said, adjusting his seat belt.

"May I see your license and registration please?" The officer asked.

Malik calmly handed the officer what he had asked for.

"Where you two headed?"

"To the library to study for an exam."

"Have a nice day," The officer said, handing him his credentials. "Looking forward to a win when we play Duke."

"Already," Malik said as he slowly pulled away, raised his window and drove off in traffic.

"Bruh, how you from the city and you playing for Carolina?" Castro started looking in Malik's direction.

"Bruh, you already know I'ma Carolina fan. It's always been a dream. Besides, Chapel Hill only thirteen miles away," Malik said with a smile.

"Fuck that. Nigga Duke in our backyard. We used to run all through that shit."

"Yeah, and they ain't have no problem locking our ass up. They don't care about us. I'm good where I'm at."

"So, where you headed now?" Castro asked.

"About to go drop this work off to my lil man."

"Who Roc Boy?"

"Yeah, why? What's good?"

"Nah, it's nothing. I'm just tryna get some of that work," Castro responded calmly.

"Shit this it. But next week this time we should be super good. Ceelo 'bout to pull up with a hundred of them thangs, and we gone move all them shits. So getcha mind right, cause it's about to go down." Malik really didn't want to go into detail about Ceelo and his operation, but he allowed him to see just enough to get him motivated.

"Bruh, that's what Jade was talking 'bout. Damn, she's making that move this weekend and shit supposed to fall Wednesday night."

Malik glanced over at Castro. It was the one piece of information he had been waiting on because he couldn't ask Jade knowing Ceelo had instructed her to remain silent concerning her plans to travel out West.

"It's time we get it how we live homie," Kream stated building self-confidence. "You see how shit just always seem to fall in our lap?"

"Wednesday ain't gone be a good time for us. We got a game remember?" Malik reminded his alter ego. "We just gotta either send the homies, or put it off till another day."

"Oh, we gone be there. Trust me...I got a plan." Kream thought to himself, treacherously grinning with excitement.

To Be Continued...

About The Author

Within the prison's wall full of malice and deceit, Marquis McKenzie sets out to climb the ladder of the impossible. In the mentoring limelight of his role model, Cash, Marquis aims to build an empire, armed with the dedication and drive of a one man army, he refuses to fail. Roadblocks appear out of thin air, his most trusted comrades forsaking him in times of need, but like a true Navy Seal he continues to fight for his life until the battle is won and his goals are achieved.

To learn more, write to:
Marquis McKenzie #0270942
TextBehind.com
Or send a message through:
GettingOut.com

Lock Down Publications and Ca$h Presents
Assisted Publishing Packages

BASIC PACKAGE	UPGRADED PACKAGE
$499	$800
Editing	Typing
Cover Design	Editing
Formatting	Cover Design
	Formatting
ADVANCE PACKAGE	**LDP SUPREME PACKAGE**
$1,200	$1,500
Typing	Typing
Editing	Editing
Cover Design	Cover Design
Formatting	Formatting
Copyright registration	Copyright registration
Proofreading	Proofreading
Upload book to Amazon	Set up Amazon account
	Upload book to Amazon
	Advertise on LDP, Amazon and Facebook Page

***Other services available upon request.
Additional charges may apply

Lock Down Publications
P.O. Box 944
Stockbridge, GA 30281-9998
Phone: 470 303-9761

Submission Guideline

Submit the first three chapters of your completed manuscript to ldpsubmissions@gmail.com. In the subject line add **Your Book's Title**. The manuscript must be in a Word Doc file and sent as an attachment. Document should be in Times New Roman, double spaced, and in size 12 font. Also, provide your synopsis and full contact information. If sending multiple submissions, they must each be in a separate email.

Have a story but no way to send it electronically? You can still submit to LDP/Ca$h Presents. Send in the first three chapters, written or typed, of your completed manuscript to:

LDP: Submissions Dept
P.O. Box 944
Stockbridge, GA 30281-9998

DO NOT send original manuscript. Must be a duplicate.
Provide your synopsis and a cover letter containing your full contact information.

Thanks for considering LDP and Ca$h Presents.

NEW RELEASES

BLOODLINE OF A SAVAGE **BY PRINCE A. TAUHID**

THE MURDER QUEENS 4 **BY MICHAEL GALLON**

THE BUTTERFLY MAFIA **BY FUMIYA PAYNE**

KING KILLA 2 **BY VINCENT "VITTO" HOLLOWAY**

BABY, I'M WINTERTIME COLD 3 **BY MEESHA**

THESE VICIOUS STREETS **BY PRINCE A. TAUHID**

TIL DEATH 2 **BY ARYANNA**

CITY OF SMOKE 2 **BY MOLOTTI**

STEPPERS **BY KING RIO**

THE LANE **BY KEN-KEN SPENCE**

MONEY GAME 2 **BY SMOOVE DOLLA**

THE BLACK DIAMOND CARTEL **BY SAYNOMORE**

CRIME BOSS 2 **BY PLAYA RAY**

THUG OF SPADES **BY COREY ROBINSON**

LOVE IN THE TRENCHES 2 **BY COREY ROBINSON**

TIL DEATH 3 **BY ARYANNA**

THE BIRTH OF A GANGSTER 4 **BY DELMONT PLAYER**

PRODUCT OF THE STREETS **BY DEMOND "MONEY" ANDERSON**

Coming Soon from Lock Down Publications/Ca$h Presents

BLOOD OF A BOSS VI
SHADOWS OF THE GAME II
TRAP BASTARD II
By **Askari**

LOYAL TO THE GAME IV
By **T.J. & Jelissa**

TRUE SAVAGE VIII
MIDNIGHT CARTEL IV
DOPE BOY MAGIC IV
CITY OF KINGZ III
NIGHTMARE ON SILENT AVE II
THE PLUG OF LIL MEXICO II
CLASSIC CITY II
By **Chris Green**

BLAST FOR ME III
A SAVAGE DOPEBOY III
CUTTHROAT MAFIA III
DUFFLE BAG CARTEL VII
HEARTLESS GOON VI
By **Ghost**

A HUSTLER'S DECEIT III
KILL ZONE II
BAE BELONGS TO ME III
TIL DEATH II
By **Aryanna**

KING OF THE TRAP III
By **T.J. Edwards**

GORILLAZ IN THE BAY V
3X KRAZY III
STRAIGHT BEAST MODE III
By **De'Kari**

KINGPIN KILLAZ IV
STREET KINGS III
PAID IN BLOOD III
CARTEL KILLAZ IV
DOPE GODS III
By **Hood Rich**

SINS OF A HUSTLA II
By **ASAD**

YAYO V
BRED IN THE GAME 2
By **S. Allen**

THE STREETS WILL TALK II
By **Yolanda Moore**

SON OF A DOPE FIEND III
HEAVEN GOT A GHETTO III
SKI MASK MONEY III
By **Renta**

LOYALTY AIN'T PROMISED III
By **Keith Williams**

I'M NOTHING WITHOUT HIS LOVE II
SINS OF A THUG II
TO THE THUG I LOVED BEFORE II
IN A HUSTLER I TRUST II
By **Monet Dragun**

QUIET MONEY IV
EXTENDED CLIP III
THUG LIFE IV
By **Trai'Quan**

THE STREETS MADE ME IV
By **Larry D. Wright**

IF YOU CROSS ME ONCE III
ANGEL V
By **Anthony Fields**

THE STREETS WILL NEVER CLOSE IV
By **K'ajji**

HARD AND RUTHLESS III
KILLA KOUNTY IV
By **Khufu**

MONEY GAME III
By **Smoove Dolla**

MURDA WAS THE CASE III
Elijah R. Freeman

AN UNFORESEEN LOVE IV
BABY, I'M WINTERTIME COLD III
By **Meesha**

QUEEN OF THE ZOO III
By **Black Migo**

CONFESSIONS OF A JACKBOY III
By **Nicholas Lock**

JACK BOYS VS DOPE BOYS IV
A GANGSTA'S QUR'AN V
COKE GIRLZ II
COKE BOYS II
LIFE OF A SAVAGE V
CHI'RAQ GANGSTAS V
SOSA GANG III
BRONX SAVAGES II
BODYMORE KINGPINS II
By **Romell Tukes**

KING KILLA II
By **Vincent "Vitto" Holloway**

BETRAYAL OF A THUG III
By **Fre$h**

THE MURDER QUEENS III
By **Michael Gallon**

THE BIRTH OF A GANGSTER III
By **Delmont Player**

TREAL LOVE II
By **Le'Monica Jackson**

FOR THE LOVE OF BLOOD III
By **Jamel Mitchell**

RAN OFF ON DA PLUG II
By **Paper Boi Rari**

HOOD CONSIGLIERE III
By **Keese**

PRETTY GIRLS DO NASTY THINGS II
By **Nicole Goosby**

PROTÉGÉ OF A LEGEND III
LOVE IN THE TRENCHES II
By **Corey Robinson**

IT'S JUST ME AND YOU II
By **Ah'Million**

FOREVER GANGSTA III
By **Adrian Dulan**

GORILLAZ IN THE TRENCHES II
By **SayNoMore**

THE COCAINE PRINCESS VIII
By **King Rio**

CRIME BOSS II
By **Playa Ray**

LOYALTY IS EVERYTHING III
By **Molotti**

HERE TODAY GONE TOMORROW II
By **Fly Rock**

REAL G'S MOVE IN SILENCE II
By **Von Diesel**

GRIMEY WAYS IV
By **Ray Vinci**

Available Now

RESTRAINING ORDER I & II
By **CA$H & Coffee**

LOVE KNOWS NO BOUNDARIES I II & III
By **Coffee**

RAISED AS A GOON I, II, III & IV
BRED BY THE SLUMS I, II, III
BLAST FOR ME I & II
ROTTEN TO THE CORE I II III
A BRONX TALE I, II, III
DUFFLE BAG CARTEL I II III IV V VI
HEARTLESS GOON I II III IV V
A SAVAGE DOPEBOY I II
DRUG LORDS I II III
CUTTHROAT MAFIA I II
KING OF THE TRENCHES
By **Ghost**

LAY IT DOWN I & II
LAST OF A DYING BREED I II
BLOOD STAINS OF A SHOTTA I & II III
By **Jamaica**

LOYAL TO THE GAME I II III
LIFE OF SIN I, II III
By **TJ & Jelissa**

IF LOVING HIM IS WRONG…I & II
LOVE ME EVEN WHEN IT HURTS I II III
By **Jelissa**

NO TIME FOR ERROR | KEESE

BLOODY COMMAS I & II
SKI MASK CARTEL I, II & III
KING OF NEW YORK I II, III IV V
RISE TO POWER I II III
COKE KINGS I II III IV V
BORN HEARTLESS I II III IV
KING OF THE TRAP I II
By **T.J. Edwards**

WHEN THE STREETS CLAP BACK I & II III
THE HEART OF A SAVAGE I II III IV
MONEY MAFIA I II
LOYAL TO THE SOIL I II III
By **Jibril Williams**

A DISTINGUISHED THUG STOLE MY HEART I II &
III
LOVE SHOULDN'T HURT I II III IV
RENEGADE BOYS I II III IV
PAID IN KARMA I II III
SAVAGE STORMS I II III
AN UNFORESEEN LOVE I II III
BABY, I'M WINTERTIME COLD I II
By **Meesha**

A GANGSTER'S CODE I &, II III
A GANGSTER'S SYN I II III
THE SAVAGE LIFE I II III
CHAINED TO THE STREETS I II III
BLOOD ON THE MONEY I II III
A GANGSTA'S PAIN I II III
By **J-Blunt**

PUSH IT TO THE LIMIT
By **Bre' Hayes**

BLOOD OF A BOSS I, II, III, IV, V
SHADOWS OF THE GAME
TRAP BASTARD
By **Askari**

THE STREETS BLEED MURDER I, II & III
THE HEART OF A GANGSTA I II& III
By **Jerry Jackson**

CUM FOR ME I II III IV V VI VII VIII
An **LDP Erotica Collaboration**

BRIDE OF A HUSTLA I II & II
THE FETTI GIRLS I, II& III
CORRUPTED BY A GANGSTA I, II III, IV
BLINDED BY HIS LOVE
THE PRICE YOU PAY FOR LOVE I, II ,III
DOPE GIRL MAGIC I II III
By **Destiny Skai**

WHEN A GOOD GIRL GOES BAD
By **Adrienne**

A GANGSTER'S REVENGE I II III & IV
THE BOSS MAN'S DAUGHTERS I II III IV V
A SAVAGE LOVE I & II
BAE BELONGS TO ME I II
A HUSTLER'S DECEIT I, II, III
WHAT BAD BITCHES DO I, II, III
SOUL OF A MONSTER I II III
KILL ZONE
A DOPE BOY'S QUEEN I II III
TIL DEATH
By **Aryanna**

THE COST OF LOYALTY I II III
By Kweli

A KINGPIN'S AMBITION
A KINGPIN'S AMBITION **II**
I MURDER FOR THE DOUGH
By **Ambitious**

TRUE SAVAGE I II III IV V VI VII
DOPE BOY MAGIC I, II, III
MIDNIGHT CARTEL I II III
CITY OF KINGZ I II
NIGHTMARE ON SILENT AVE
THE PLUG OF LIL MEXICO II
CLASSIC CITY
By **Chris Green**

A DOPEBOY'S PRAYER
By **Eddie "Wolf" Lee**

THE KING CARTEL I, II & III
By **Frank Gresham**

THESE NIGGAS AIN'T LOYAL I, II & III
By **Nikki Tee**

GANGSTA SHYT I II &III
By **CATO**

THE ULTIMATE BETRAYAL
By **Phoenix**

BOSS'N UP I, II & III
By **Royal Nicole**

NO TIME FOR ERROR | KEESE

I LOVE YOU TO DEATH
By **Destiny J**

I RIDE FOR MY HITTA
I STILL RIDE FOR MY HITTA
By **Misty Holt**

LOVE & CHASIN' PAPER
By **Qay Crockett**

TO DIE IN VAIN
SINS OF A HUSTLA
By **ASAD**

BROOKLYN HUSTLAZ
By **Boogsy Morina**

BROOKLYN ON LOCK I & II
By **Sonovia**

GANGSTA CITY
By **Teddy Duke**

A DRUG KING AND HIS DIAMOND I & II III
A DOPEMAN'S RICHES
HER MAN, MINE'S TOO I, II
CASH MONEY HO'S
THE WIFEY I USED TO BE I II
PRETTY GIRLS DO NASTY THINGS
By Nicole Goosby

LIPSTICK KILLAH I, II, III
CRIME OF PASSION I II & III
FRIEND OR FOE I II III
By **Mimi**

TRAPHOUSE KING I II & III
KINGPIN KILLAZ I II III
STREET KINGS I II
PAID IN BLOOD I II
CARTEL KILLAZ I II III
DOPE GODS I II
By **Hood Rich**

STEADY MOBBN' I, II, III
THE STREETS STAINED MY SOUL I II III
By **Marcellus Allen**

WHO SHOT YA I, II, III
SON OF A DOPE FIEND I II
HEAVEN GOT A GHETTO I II
SKI MASK MONEY I II
By **Renta**

GORILLAZ IN THE BAY I II III IV
TEARS OF A GANGSTA I II
3X KRAZY I II
STRAIGHT BEAST MODE I II
By **DE'KARI**

TRIGGADALE I II III
MURDA WAS THE CASE I II
By **Elijah R. Freeman**

THE STREETS ARE CALLING
By **Duquie Wilson**

SLAUGHTER GANG I II III
RUTHLESS HEART I II III
By **Willie Slaughter**

NO TIME FOR ERROR | KEESE

GOD BLESS THE TRAPPERS I, II, III
THESE SCANDALOUS STREETS I, II, III
FEAR MY GANGSTA I, II, III IV, V
THESE STREETS DON'T LOVE NOBODY I, II
BURY ME A G I, II, III, IV, V
A GANGSTA'S EMPIRE I, II, III, IV
THE DOPEMAN'S BODYGAURD I II
THE REALEST KILLAZ I II III
THE LAST OF THE OGS I II III
By **Tranay Adams**

MARRIED TO A BOSS I II III
By **Destiny Skai & Chris Green**

KINGZ OF THE GAME I II III IV V VI VII
CRIME BOSS
By **Playa Ray**

FUK SHYT
By **Blakk Diamond**

DON'T F#CK WITH MY HEART I II
By **Linnea**

ADDICTED TO THE DRAMA I II III
IN THE ARM OF HIS BOSS II
By **Jamila**

YAYO I II III IV
A SHOOTER'S AMBITION I II
BRED IN THE GAME
By **S. Allen**

LOYALTY AIN'T PROMISED I II
By **Keith Williams**

153

TRAP GOD I II III
RICH $AVAGE I II III
MONEY IN THE GRAVE I II III
By **Martell Troublesome Bolden**

FOREVER GANGSTA I II
GLOCKS ON SATIN SHEETS I II
By **Adrian Dulan**

TOE TAGZ I II III IV
LEVELS TO THIS SHYT I II
IT'S JUST ME AND YOU
By **Ah'Million**

KINGPIN DREAMS I II III
RAN OFF ON DA PLUG
By **Paper Boi Rari**

CONFESSIONS OF A GANGSTA I II III IV
CONFESSIONS OF A JACKBOY I II
By **Nicholas Lock**

I'M NOTHING WITHOUT HIS LOVE
SINS OF A THUG
TO THE THUG I LOVED BEFORE
A GANGSTA SAVED XMAS
IN A HUSTLER I TRUST
By **Monet Dragun**

QUIET MONEY I II III
THUG LIFE I II III
EXTENDED CLIP I II
A GANGSTA'S PARADISE
By **Trai'Quan**

CAUGHT UP IN THE LIFE I II III
THE STREETS NEVER LET GO I II III
By **Robert Baptiste**

NEW TO THE GAME I II III
MONEY, MURDER & MEMORIES I II III
By **Malik D. Rice**

CREAM I II III
THE STREETS WILL TALK
By **Yolanda Moore**

LIFE OF A SAVAGE I II III IV
A GANGSTA'S QUR'AN I II III IV
MURDA SEASON I II III
GANGLAND CARTEL I II III
CHI'RAQ GANGSTAS I II III IV
KILLERS ON ELM STREET I II III
JACK BOYZ N DA BRONX I II III
A DOPEBOY'S DREAM I II III
JACK BOYS VS DOPE BOYS I II III
COKE GIRLZ
COKE BOYS
SOSA GANG I II
BRONX SAVAGES
BODYMORE KINGPINS
By **Romell Tukes**

THE STREETS MADE ME I II III
By **Larry D. Wright**

CONCRETE KILLA I II III
VICIOUS LOYALTY I II III
By **Kingpen**

THE ULTIMATE SACRIFICE I, II, III, IV, V, VI
KHADIFI
IF YOU CROSS ME ONCE I II
ANGEL I II III IV
IN THE BLINK OF AN EYE
By **Anthony Fields**

THE LIFE OF A HOOD STAR
By **Ca$h & Rashia Wilson**

THE STREETS WILL NEVER CLOSE I II III
By **K'ajji**

NIGHTMARES OF A HUSTLA I II III
By **King Dream**

HARD AND RUTHLESS I II
MOB TOWN 251
THE BILLIONAIRE BENTLEYS I II III
REAL G'S MOVE IN SILENCE
By **Von Diesel**

GHOST MOB
By **Stilloan Robinson**

MOB TIES I II III IV V VI
SOUL OF A HUSTLER, HEART OF A KILLER I II
GORILLAZ IN THE TRENCHES
By **SayNoMore**

BODYMORE MURDERLAND I II III
THE BIRTH OF A GANGSTER I II
By **Delmont Player**

NO TIME FOR ERROR | KEESE

FOR THE LOVE OF A BOSS
By **C. D. Blue**

KILLA KOUNTY I II III IV
By Khufu

MOBBED UP I II III IV
THE BRICK MAN I II III IV V
THE COCAINE PRINCESS I II III IV V VI VII
By **King Rio**

MONEY GAME I II
By **Smoove Dolla**

A GANGSTA'S KARMA I II III
By **FLAME**

KING OF THE TRENCHES I II III
By **GHOST & TRANAY ADAMS**

QUEEN OF THE ZOO I II
By **Black Migo**

GRIMEY WAYS I II III
By **Ray Vinci**

XMAS WITH AN ATL SHOOTER
By **Ca$h & Destiny Skai**

KING KILLA
By **Vincent "Vitto" Holloway**

BETRAYAL OF A THUG I II
By **Fre$h**

NO TIME FOR ERROR | KEESE

THE MURDER QUEENS I II
By **Michael Gallon**

TREAL LOVE
By **Le'Monica Jackson**

FOR THE LOVE OF BLOOD I II
By **Jamel Mitchell**

HOOD CONSIGLIERE I II
By **Keese**

PROTÉGÉ OF A LEGEND I II
LOVE IN THE TRENCHES
By **Corey Robinson**

BORN IN THE GRAVE I II III
By **Self Made Tay**

MOAN IN MY MOUTH
By **XTASY**

TORN BETWEEN A GANGSTER AND A
GENTLEMAN
By **J-BLUNT & Miss Kim**

LOYALTY IS EVERYTHING I II
By **Molotti**

HERE TODAY GONE TOMORROW
By **Fly Rock**

PILLOW PRINCESS
By **S. Hawkins**

NO TIME FOR ERROR | KEESE

SANCTIFIED AND HORNY
by **XTASY**

THE PLUG OF LIL MEXICO 2
by **CHRIS GREEN**

THE BLACK DIAMOND CARTEL
by **SAYNOMORE**

THE BIRTH OF A GANGSTER 3
by **DELMONT PLAYER**

BOOKS BY LDP'S CEO, CA$H

TRUST IN NO MAN
TRUST IN NO MAN 2
TRUST IN NO MAN 3
BONDED BY BLOOD
SHORTY GOT A THUG
THUGS CRY
THUGS CRY 2
THUGS CRY 3
TRUST NO BITCH
TRUST NO BITCH 2
TRUST NO BITCH 3
TIL MY CASKET DROPS
RESTRAINING ORDER
RESTRAINING ORDER 2
IN LOVE WITH A CONVICT
LIFE OF A HOOD STAR
XMAS WITH AN ATL SHOOTER